Love...

Better late than never

Love...

Better late than never

Deepika Behal

PARTRIDGE

A Penguin Random House Company

Print information available on the last page.

To order additional copies of this book, contact
Partridge India
000 800 10062 62
orders.india@partridgepublishing.com

www.partridgepublishing.com/india

To my Mom & Dad...my two shining stars, who've guided me all the way.

CONTENTS

CHAPTER 1

It was a brilliant early morning, birds chirped, light breeze ruffled the leaves and played with the wind chimes in the balcony; sunrays beamed through the huge bay windows of the wide room, adorned lavishly, walls covered in baby pink; complete with a walk-in closet filled with best clothes, shoes and bags money could buy. A room fit for a Princess to live in and a Princess, she was.

Aadvi Kapoor, Princess of the Kapoor Mansion, the only daughter of telecom hotshot and sole heiress to the multi-millionaire Rajan Kapoor's fortune. Aadvi was adored by one and all, the apple of her Mom's eyes, darling of her father. Such was her charm that her mere presence was enough to uplift their mood.

She was like an angelic blessing…deep brown eyes, fair skin, tall, delicate, voluptuous body, a sweet voice and a calm attitude, beauty second only to that of fairies, except that fairies were unreal, unlike her. But in spite of the riches, her feet were firmly grounded, for she knew her father had worked hard for the money and despite being a part of a money minded, gold digging society she was a humble girl deep down. She had done what other girls of such highflying families generally don't accomplish at such a young age.

Aadvi was smart, savvy and driven; having completed her studies from Oxford University in England she assisted her hotelier uncle to support herself.

An achiever, at the vibrant age of 25, she was now a smart and intelligent young businesswoman, working actively as one of directors in MobiVoice, the company founded by her father.

She helped out her mother often with her charity work besides being a dedicated Rotarian and Paul Harris fellow, just like her father.

Rajan Kapoor, youngest son of the Late Lala Dashrath Kapoor and Late Sharda Kapoor who settled in Delhi after the partition with Rajan's grand parents. Born and brought up in Delhi Rajan was the younger of the two brothers. A brilliant student in his school time, Rajan always dreamt big. A post-graduate from the Massachusetts Institute of Technology a devoted husband and a doting father.

For Rajan family had always been his top most priority. Despite being a busy man, he made sure he spent time with his wife, gave ample time to his daughter…made sure to be present for the birthday's, the annual day functions, or the school plays, he was always around for the family.

Rajan loved to travel and that rubbed off on Aadvi too. The wanderlust had got her at an early age. She accompanied her parents everywhere, even on the business trips. Now sisnce she was working with her father, she had traveled extensively around the globe. An avid nature lover and great cook, she loved to read. She also found solace in music and had soulful voice having trained since the tender age of five.

But everything was not rosy in her otherwise perfect world.

She had everything a girl could ask for, except for love.

She was still on the lookout for her ideal man. She envisioned her man, like any other normal girl, someone who could love her from the core of his heart.

"Wake up, darling, rise and shine" called a voice, which was like music to everyone's ears in Kapoor mansion.

A woman with a divine smile on her face, wearing turquoise colored Sari, stood next to Aadvi's bed…Preeti Kapoor, Aadvi's mother and Rajan's better half.

Preeti was an ideal daughter to an industrialist father, dutiful wife to a tycoon husband and a loving mother to a beautiful daughter. Preeti was a perfect housewife. She used to work with Rajan during the initial years after the marriage but was now a dedicated housewife, who like any other woman loved to take care of her family, pamper them, scold them, control them.

A pious lady and a typical Indian housewife, she got up early in the morning, offered prayers in the huge temple specially built inside the premises of the mansion. Now happily settled in domesticity she ran an army of domestic help around the house. She did a lot of charity work and also funded a shelter for homeless women.

Like every other mother she wanted her daughter to get settled. She firmly believed that God would eventually send her prince, a man worthy of her loving her princess.

Aadvi woke up, rubbing her eyes, and looked at her mother who was still as beautiful as she was the day she got married.

"My, My, someone's looking beautiful this morning?"

"And why shouldn't I? It's a special day...don't you remember?" she asked handing over a bowl of Aadvi's favorite cereal as she cut some fresh fruits for her.

"What is it, tell me?" Aadvi scratched her head.

"It's *Naanu's* birthday today!" Preeti informed her.

Naanu was Aadvi's maternal grandfather, Mr.Ramdass Chopra, a well reputed businessman of his times, now retired as his health did not allow him to work. A grieving widower, Mr.Chopra lost the love of his life, his wife, Lajwanti to cardiac arrest, a few years ago. Aadvi was his only grandchild from Preeti his daughter, since his teenaged son Ramesh Chopra died in an accident while on a college trip. So naturally his love for Aadvi knew no bounds and loved her to the core. He could never refuse Aadvi for anything. Her every wish was his command.

She continued eating her breakfast, which was served in bed that morning, and was a rarity in itself, as Preeti never spoilt her daughter. Breakfast or for that matter any meal was meant to have sitting together as a family in the dining room. But that morning was exceptional as Rajan left early for the office and Preeti and Aadvi were to leave for the Chopra Estate in Meherauli.

Aadvi pointed a finger towards a rectangular box placed next to the window, gift wrapped in a golden paper and smiled impishly looking at her mother.

"Look there!"

"What's that?"

"*Naanu's* gift! Have I ever forgotten anything about him…I was kidding Mom"

"That's like my girl…ok now hurry up and get ready, we have to make a move towards *Naanu's* house"

"Ok Mom"

She hurried out of the bed and headed for shower. She decided to drive the car herself. A customized Bentley designed specially and gifted to the Princess, as Rajan fondly called Aadvi, on her 23rd, headed towards the posh area of Meherauli where his ever-faithful butler ran Gurmeet's son Joginder Mr.Chopra's palatial Estate. As the car entered the Estate, the guards at the gate saluted them.

They proceeded towards the living room where Joginder recieved them in his usual graceful manner.

"Hello Preeti mam, Aadvi mam, how are you doing this morning?"

"We are fine Joginder, but where is Papa, hope he had his medicines on time this morning?"

"Sir is in his room, and I personally make sure everyday that he takes his medicines on time, my father guided me to serve him at every moment, when I joined the Estate" he paused to clear his throat as he remembered his father whom he recently lost in a train mishap, "Shall I inform him of your arrival?" Preeti consoled him.

"We are very sorry for your loss Joginder, Gurmeet ji was a Nobel man."

Joginder collected himself.

"And don't worry we are here to surprise Papa, could you please have somebody get his gift from the car!"

"Sure Preeti mam, please carry on. I'll send it right away!"

They walked towards Mr.Chopra's room on the first floor where a stocky old man, with wrinkled skin, white moustache, dressed in white tees and grey sweatpants, sat on a couch, looking at his late wife's Lajwanti's portrait hanging on the wall. With a fleeting look of despair on his face, he reminisced the good old days when he used to celebrate his birthday with a lot of pomp with his wife, kids and loved one's in the midst.

Just then Aadvi entered the room with Preeti and found her beloved Grand father with tear filled eyes. She gently wiped the tears and sang him Happy Birthday in her melodious voice.

"*Naanu* I know you miss *Naani* but she would never would've liked to see you cry like this, that too on such a special day."

"I am sorry, but her absence makes me sad, having lived my entire life with her, sharing the best and the worst, my journey from rags to riches, my kids being born, everything reminds me for her" he paused for a while "but yeah I have get over it and I will try, but for now, where is my gift?"

"Right there…" she directed his attention towards a box being placed by a helper in the corner of the room.

Mr. Chopra sat on his wheelchair as Aadvi took him to the box. He unwrapped it and found an old picture of him and his wife, from their honeymoon in Kashmir, in an antique golden frame.

"Thank you darling! Couldn't have received a better gift than this, God Bless You!" He blessed her, kissing her forehead.

Giving him a tight hug and peck on the cheek, "ok *Naanu*, I have to get going, have to reach the office on time, Dad would be waiting for me, and have to discuss some plans for our new mobile plant in Faridabad."

"Go ahead, but remember, like you find time for your meetings try finding yourself a husband, you have to get married before I set in for the long nap,"

"*Naanu*! Please stop it… one thing at a time, and don't say all these things, at least not today…take care of him mother, I'll see you lovelies in the evening…Bye" Aadvi left the room waving towards them.

"Bye sweetheart" as they both wave her goodbye; Preeti took a seat next to her father on the sofa.

"Preeti, Rajan called me this morning to wish me, in fact he was the first one…I am grateful to the almighty for such a son-in-law, God Bless him."

She smiled; admiring her father who exuded nothing but love and showered blessings on everyone but also felt the pain of lonesomeness in his eyes since her mother passed away.

"Preeti, have you started looking for potential suitors for Aadvi, its high time she settles down, and like I said I would like to see her tie the knot before…"

Preeti stopped him.

"Papa before you go any further, may God Bless you with a long life and yes we are looking for suitable boys for her and Rajan too has been keeping an eye in the business circle, in fact he likes a boy too, but the only problem is how do we speak to his parents?"

"Why, what seems to be the problem?"

"Actually, the boy in question is the son of an old friend of Rajan's, and we lost touch with them, now how do we talk to him is the question as it's the responsibility of the elders of the family to get involved in these things and like you know Rajan's parents are no more." after a pause she continued "actually, Rajan wanted to speak to you, if you could talk on our behalf, to his friend regarding this relationship."

"What does the boy do, how is the family?"

"The boy's name is Akash, Aadvi knows him since childhood, they both were good friends. His father Inderjeet Khanna and mother Roma were Rajan's batch mates at MIT."

"Akash completed his MBA from Stern School in New York and came back last year. He is now working with his father in their hotel business. His parents were very close to us but then they shifted to Mumbai for business expansion and we just lost touch."

"Aadvi was growing up while I concentrated on her, Rajan was caught up in his work. But they've just come back to Delhi a few months ago and we have been in touch with each other recently."

"Well if the family is good and you both are satisfied, I will surely talk to them. Why don't you ask Rajan to invite them for the party this evening and tell them that I insist on their presence."

Preeti picked up the phone and called Rajan.

"Hello, Rajan Kapoor."

"Rajan, Preeti this side, I am sitting with Papa and he wishes to speak to you."

"Yeah sure, hope he is fine!"

"Yes he's fine, just speak to him."

Mr.Chopra took the phone from Preeti, "Hello Rajan, son why didn't you tell me about Akash and his family when you called me this morning. I will surely speak to them regarding Aadvi and Akash's marriage. Why don't you invite them for the party this evening?"

"Papa, I didn't want to bother you since you were as it is emotional about Ramesh and Mom. But if you insist I will call Inderjeet and invite him, but I would advise you meet them first, convey the idea to Aadvi and then go ahead."

"Sounds right, ok then. But insist on Akash's presence. I want to meet him too."

"Alright Papa…see you in the evening."

Rajan called Inderjeet at his office.

"Hello, Inder, Rajan Kapoor this side!"

"Oh Hello Rajan, how are you?"

"I am fine, how is Roma and how is your son, must've turned out to be as handsome as you are."

"Yes he has surely turned out to be a head turner, Roma is amazing as ever, lucky to have her, I look at her everyday and thank my stars, that I took your advice and asked her out before that jerk Brandon…anyway, how is Preeti and Aadvi our little angel?"

"The little angel is all grown up now turned out to be as beautiful as her mother, Preeti, is my lucky charm, her luck changed my fortunes and her beauty still has me charmed!"

"True…you both are lucky to have each other."

"Inder…I wanted to invite you over this evening…it's my father-in-law's 75th birthday and we are celebrating after a long time almost 5 years since my mother-in-law passed away. He didn't want to celebrate, but Aadvi insisted we do. So, she's arranged a party, and you have to be there with Roma and Akash."

"Alright Rajan, we'll be there, just tell me the time and venue."

"Hotel Maharaja, poolside, 8 pm …looking forward to seeing you."

Chapter 2

8:30 pm, Hotel Maharaja, the poolside was bustling, the guests were pouring in and the party was in full swing. Champagne flowed and piping hot *tikkas*, *kebabs* and other hors d'oeuvres were being served around, the musical troupe flown is specially from Mumbai was playing the choicest of Romantic numbers from the Golden era of Hindi cinema. Subtle lighting and fresh flowers enhanced the ambience.

Aadvi looked ravishing as ever in a gorgeous Versace, backless, black sequin gown with black Manolo Blahnik pumps, her long lustrous hair flowed on back and even with limited make-up she looked stunning.

Being the hostess of the party, she was personally looking after the arrangements and the guests.

Despite 28 years of marriage, Rajan and Preeti made a handsome couple. Rajan even at the age of 55 looked no more than forty, a well maintained man, he looked handsome as ever in black three piece Armani suit and his better half, Preeti looked fabulous in red and gold embellished sari. They eagerly awaited, Inderjeet and Roma's arrival.

Finally after much deliberation, Inderjeet Khanna arrived at the party with wife Roma and son Akash in tow.

Akash Khanna…oh that dream of a guy, every girl hoped of finding one day, tall, sensual, poised, brown hair, light brown eyes, lightly tanned skin, light stubble, looking dapper in a two piece suit and to that add a charming persona, he was quiet the package.

But beyond the attractive looks, he was the ideal son to Inderjeet Khanna, the pot bellied friend of Rajan, a high flying businessman and an Hotelier in a gray suit along with his wife Roma, wearing an emerald colored sari. A one-time businesswoman turned a part time author to a full time mother of to a fine-looking son.

Though he was not a hardcore party animal but wasn't a recluse either. A cricket lover and tennis player himself his other passions included music and he strummed the strings at times.

But this fish had already been caught. Akash was already in a relationship with an American model, Andrea Johnson, back in the United States, a fact everyone was unaware of.

Since coming back from the Big Apple two years ago, finishing his Masters in Business Administration, he was now learning the tricks of the trade from his father. The long distance relation was still working out though. At least he was trying to make it work. He made a point to call Andrea everyday and also visit her whenever possible.

He intended to talk to his parents about Andrea, as he wanted to propose her as soon as possible, but was quiet about it since, Andrea was busy making her career and he too was trying to settle in his father's business.

Rajan and Preeti, greeted Inderjeet, Roma, as they entered with a big bouquet of the finest lilies, held by Akash. Akash touched Rajan and Preeti's feet as a mark of respect in the Indian culture.

"God Bless You son…" Rajan hugged him and then focused his attention on Inderjeet whom he had met after a long time, "Inder, old buddy, thank you for coming, it really means a lot to us, but why did you come so late?"

"An urgent meeting came up at the last minute, rushed here as soon as I got free. So glad to see you *yarra*…thank you for inviting us over Rajan, great party, hope you won't be caught up in this soiree and will be able to share a drink or two with your old friend?"

"I am never too busy for my family *Prah*, let's hit the bar!" Rajan was excited.

While the women exchanged pleasantries, men continued their talks.

"Rajan, but first introduce us to Mr.Chopra and let us wish him!"

"Yes, come I'll introduce you to him.

All of them walked towards Mr.Chopra who sat in the company of his friends, sharing a glass of wine.

"Papa, I'd like you to meet Inderjeet Khanna, my very dear friend."

"Welcome to the party *puttar*, I am glad you could come."

"Thank you for having us over uncle, wish you a very Happy Birthday, my wife Roma and my son Akash."

Inderjeet introduced his wife and son standing behind him as Roma and Akash presented him the bouquet and touched Mr.Chopra's feet.

As he blessed them, he paused and looked at Akash. He asked Joginder, who stood next to him, to look for Aadvi.

Joginder looked around for Aadvi, whom he saw sitting with a group of friends, chatting away. She didn't have a large group of friends, as she didn't have much of a social life after school. Such occasions were the times when she caught up with the remaining lot.

"Aadvi mam, Chopra Sir is calling you."

Aadvi promptly went to see her *Naanu* and while walking towards him, an attractive guy, standing next to her father caught her attention.

Is he really who I think he is?

Rajan introduced Aadvi to Inderjeet's family

"Aadvi, meet Inderjeet uncle and Roma aunty and their son Akash…remember him."

"Hello uncle, aunty."

Then turned her face towards the hunk standing in front; her heart fluttered with anticipation.

It's really him!

Preeti noticed Aadvi's reaction, "Rajan, I think Aadvi has forgotten him…don't you remember him Aadvi, you were such good friends, we used to go for holidays every summer."

She knew who Akash was. He was her friend with whom she spent great times as a kid. They practically grew up together. At a point in time, she even had a crush on him. They were still in their mid teens when Akash left for Mumbai with his parents.

"Of course I remember him, it's not been so long that I'll forget my childhood friend…that too such a naughty one."

"Hi Akash…I am seeing you after ages!"

He looked back at her with those intense; piercing eyes… she felt hypnotized.

"Hello Aadvi, yeah it's been a long time, almost ten years."

Meanwhile Mr.Chopra could see the great pair that Aadvi and Akash would make. Being a man with a world of knowledge, he could see that Akash would be perfect one for his grand daughter. He asked Aadvi to, take Akash, show him around introduce him to friends and family, which she gladly does, not knowing the purpose behind the deliberate effort.

Rajan and Inderjeet headed to the bar discussing business as the ladies got seated recalling the good old days.

The night was still young and Aadvi, the most eligible young woman in the city walked next to the most desirable man in the crowd. They walked towards the bar. Akash got himself some wine and a vodka martini for Aadvi.

"Akash come, I'll introduce you to my friends." Aadvi pointed towards a group of young women. She was still coy.

"Lead the way."

They made their way towards her group of friends, where she introduced him to everyone, especially Avantika, her best friend from school and her confidant. Avantika Shah was confident, young girl, from a simple background as her father was an acquaintance of the Kapoor's and was a teacher of Mathematics at the same high school Aadvi and Avantika studied at.

Avantika now worked as an executive at a multinational company in Gurgaon. Recently engaged to her high school sweetheart Rajesh, she was soon to get married and ready to move to Australia with her beau.

"Akash, this is Avantika, who is more like a sister than a friend to me."

"Hey Avantika."

"Hello."

"Avantika, Akash is an childhood buddy, remember, my friend I used to tell you about about, the one I used to go on holiday with our parents."

Avantika could now recall. Aadvi had mentioned his name many at times, but nothing much.

Aadvi and Avantika had been friends through thick and thin. Avantika knew how empty Aadvi felt from inside, despite having everything. Today it was different; she couldn't help but notice a spark of joy in Aadvi's eyes.

There was something about Akash, which made Aadvi more inquisitive about him. Despite knowing him from childhood having spent a good amount of time with him; she never felt the way she did now.

Childhood, a passing phase where people come in our lives and people leave too, she could never imagine someone she long lost touch with, and someone she remembered as a naughty, boy who used to pick on her, pull her pig tails, made her cry, fought with her at times, could turn out to be so cool, composed and to top it all, attractive.

They had separated in their mid teens and were now meeting like this, when she had turned into a striking woman and he was now a suave young man albeit committed. Aadvi was unaware of this fact and thus her curiosity about him grew every minute.

They alienated themselves from the crowd as Akash lead her towards some empty chairs. She was excited to finally get some time alone with him. She looked intently at him as he sipped his drink.

"You've had quiet a makeover since your pigtail days Aadvi!" he smirked

"My my look who's talking...you too have turned out to be a so stylish, Mr. Khanna...quiet a makeover since your wild child phase...Nice Suit by the way!"

"Thanks a lot...it's Dior, got it from Italy last year!"

Oh God! Some things never change...like him and his fetish with brands

Akash had been a brand freak, which irritated Aadvi, even when they were young.

"Oh God you are still the same Akash deep down...still that nagging obsession with brands!"

"Well...if you've got it, flaunt it!"
"So how was America?"

"Haven't you heard, when in Rome, do as the Romans do… took to the American lifestyle like a fish to water, America really changed me. After I left Delhi for Mumbai I was quiet skeptical about how I'll manage or fit in, but slowly came to liking the place, same with New York, I didn't want to go but Dad insisted, with time, I seemed to fit in. I had a great group of friends, plus living alone teaches you a lot, makes you independent and responsible."

"And you've always wanted to be independent…I still remember, you fought with your Dad on numerous occasions to let you go to that boarding school in Nainital, with your friend, that porky guy, what was his name?"

"Raghu, short for Raghavendra…well porky is settled in U.S. as well, runs a chain of motels."

"Yeah Raghu…anyway glad to see you are a changed man, much calmer and look sophisticated too," she tried to be impish.

"So tell me about yourself Aadvi, how's life treating you?"

"Ploughing through…" she laughed,"Just kidding…well, I have great parents, lovely friends, such a wonderful grandfather, by God's grace, all in all…life is good."

"That's good to know…so are you still into the boy band kind of music or have you matured enough." he asked with a cheeky grin, "I remember how crazy you were for Backstreet Boys and Boyzone."

"Oh yeah, definitely over that phase...you got to change with times. I love Keane, Ed Sheeran, Coldplay, and old Hindi songs. Nothing beats Manna Dey, Rafi, Mukesh, Kishore, Lata, Asha..."

"Hold it hold it, that's quiet a list, I know God doesn't make singers like them anymore, I like old Hindi film songs too."

"Music is my weakness!"

"Do you still sing?"

"Not anymore...don't have the time!"

"I heard you are working with Rajan Uncle, now?"

"Yes, been working with him for quiet some time now and but I plan to start something on my own soon."

"That's good...besides work, what do you do to unwind?"

"Given my schedule, I hardly get any time, but I do travel with Dad a lot, so that itself relaxes me. I try catch up on new T.V. Shows or movies every once in a while, since I can't go out that much, Dad got a small theater constructed for family and friends where we catch up on the movies old and new."

Her eyes were still fixed on his charismatic face.

Wow, he's turned out to be such a charmer, can't believe he's the same guy who used to irritate me so much when we were kids.

"That's good…so tell me Aadvi…are you seeing anybody, any one special in your life?"

Her heart constantly pounded like drum. It was not what he had asked but how he had asked.

Oh my God! Is my wait finally over?

The bizarre conversation with the dishy man she barely knew now but wanted to more off was playing games with her usually practical mind.

"No, not yet!"

The band continued to play, taking some requests from the guests; while the lead vocalist crooned the classic, Romantic song, Yeh Raat Bheegi Bheegi, all the couples were requested to join the dance floor.

Akash looked at Aadvi and how amazing she looked.

"Can I have this dance with you?"

"Sure!"

Akash lead her to the dance floor. They began slow dancing; both of them gazed at each other, Aadvi was totally lost in that magical moment, staring in his eyes and Akash admired her elegant face.

"It's strange!" he pondered.

"What's so strange?"

"You are an amazing girl, fabulous looking, funny, rich, only an idiot would miss a chance to be with you!"

As he turned her, the moonlight, enhanced her luminous beauty all the more.

"Unfortunately, I haven't found my idiot so far?" she said with a hopeful twinkle in her eyes.

"What about you?"

She dreaded the answer…but had to face it anyway!

"Yes, I am, seeing someone back in NYC."

She was surprised…and hurt!

As though her brittle shoulders had been levied with heavy burden.

He swirled her around as they continued dancing. Mr.Chopra's eyes fixated on them amidst murmurs about the handsome looking 'couple' on the dance-floor.

Her fear had come true; the dreamy guy had been left for dreams only. But she had to brave up, mask her feelings, try and hide that spark which had been ignited in her heart already.

Gazing in his deep and intense eyes Aadvi's throat tightened more and more. She just couldn't take her eyes of him.

"That's great, who is the lucky one?" she tried her best to cover up her shock.

"Her name is Andrea, she's a model, I met her at a fashion show three years ago. I was attending it, where my friend Gustav was showing his latest his collection. She was the showstopper and from the ramp she walked right into my heart. One look at her and it was head over heels." he sighed, "The attraction was mutual when Gustav introduced us after the party. We have been dating ever since."

Aadvi's heart fell into her stomach. She braved the feeling though.

"What about wedding, any news on the D-Day?"

A question she didn't want to ask but had to…an answer she wasn't hoping to hear, but she had to.

The song faded out, the band received rousing applause as Akash and Aadvi moved towards their chairs.

"No news on that front, as I don't know how to tell my parents about her, besides that Andrea is very busy, modeling takes her around the world, but the biggest challenge to make her quit it, because my parents being typical Punjabi's won't allow their daughter-in-law to walk the ramp or be on the cover of some magazine…it's going to be one hell of a challenge."

"And would you prefer it?"

"Me ...Oh yes I am fine with it...though I do dream of a happy married life and would want my partner to be more of a home maker...I will never ask her to compromise her dreams for mine, but you never know she might just settle into that life and quit...if God willing we get married soon"

"I wish you good luck."

"Thanks, I hope you find someone soon too, love is a special feeling."

And who would know it better than Aadvi, one who had eternally craved for that feeling of being in love? For most guys, either she was too rich or too gorgeous...in any case beyond their reach.

Aadvi's parents, called for her. They moved towards the dinner tables, which had been laid out. There was no cake to cut, as Mr.Chopra didn't want to have one.

Through with the dinner soon, Aadvi and Akash exchange their numbers. The Khanna's took leave and as they moved towards the exit, Akash suddenly turned around and asked her, "Do you play Golf?

"Yes, I do!" She replied.

"Would you like to go for a round of golf at the Qutab Golf Course this Sunday?"

"Sure I would love to."

"Great, I'll pick you up around 11!"

"Sounds good."

Akash looked back to wave her goodbye…Aadvi was happy to have found a good friend, although she wanted more.

After the party winds up, she had a chance to sit with *Naanu*.

"So Aadvi how was your meeting with Akash after so many years?"

"He is a nice guy *Naanu*!" she said smiling timidly, "anyway *Naanu*, time for you to leave now."

"Yes it is…it was a tiring affair, but I am glad everyone made it…Thanks for the party, Princess."

She and Joginder took Mr.Chopra towards his car. After seeing him off, she headed for home with Preeti. Once she hit the bed, her droopy eyes began reminiscing whatever had happened that night and the 'known stranger' she had met.

CHAPTER 3

The next day, Rajan was taking it easy after the party last night. It was a sunny Friday morning; he came down from his room, joined Aadvi and Preeti in the kitchen. He looked at Preeti inquisitively, if she had spoken to Aadvi about Akash. She shook her head.

Rajan asked Aadvi to take a seat next to him as she poured him a cup of black coffee.

"Aadvi, I spoke to *Naanu* regarding Akash and you!"

She almost spilled her coffee in amazement.

"We like Akash and would like you to consider marrying him, *Naanu* will speak to Inderjeet and his wife and I am sure they won't say no since they liked you very much last night and Akash to showed a lot of interest in you plus you both will make a lovely couple."

"Dad...please stop...before you go any further, I would like to 'enlighten' you on the present situation."

Rajan looked bemused.

She took a deep breath and conveyed the news to her father, "Akash already has a steady girlfriend back in New York and he plans on proposing her soon…although he hasn't told his parents about it, since he isn't sure how they'll react to it, when they get to know that she is a model."

"I have known Inder for almost 30 years, I know he will never accept a girl from another culture let alone a model from another country, he has a very traditional mindset. If we speak to him regarding this, he'll talk Akash out of it."

"But Dad, even if we do get married, I can't be happy with him, knowing he is in love with someone else."

"Darling, please let me handle this, trust your father!"

Although reluctant at first, she decided to give her father a chance.

Aadvi was still smitten with Akash; despite knowing he was in a committed relationship.

Was it really possible…could it really happen, could she make inroads in to Akash's life and heart by marrying him, whom she had only met a few hours ago and instantly fell in love with. It was happening all too soon and Aadvi was getting panicky by the minute.

Time was ticking, and by noon, Rajan and Preeti after a long discussion with Mr.Chopra decided to speak to Inderjeet. Rajan called him.

"Hello Inder, Rajan this side."

"Hello Rajan, it was a great party last night, Roma was so happy to see all of you."

"Yes it was great catching up after so many years...Inder..." Rajan was a little hesitant.

"Come on Rajan, tell me, what is it?"

"Myself and Preeti wanted to meet you, is it possible to see you today?"

"You are most welcome Rajan but I hope everything is fine?"

"Yes everything is fine, it's something better discussed face to face."

"Sure Rajan, but I have some clients over from Singapore so I am a little tied up till Saturday, if it's important shall I cancel the appointments?"

"Oh no, please finish you work, I don't want to disturb you, we can meet on Monday then."

"Alright Rajan, see you on Monday then, bring Aadvi along too, Akash was talking about her this morning, he told me they are going for Golf on Sunday."

"Oh really, why don't we go for a round as well?"

"Sounds great, see you on Sunday then."

Avantika called Aadvi the same evening, inquiring about the stud she introduced last night. Aadvi gave her an update on what had happened so far. Avantika tried to console Aadvi, whose voice had begun to crack by then, she knew Aadvi had been crying and could sense the pain of her friend with whom she had been for the last 15 years.

She tried to pacify her, "Aadvi, relax and stop being so cynical…only time will tell what will happen and you don't need to worry about anything, your father will take care of everything. Knowing him I can vouch for the fact that he will never make a decision knowing it's not right for you. Akash wants to propose her, but hasn't done it so far, if it were to happen it could've happened by now"

"But, looking at the way things are, he is too serious about her, Avantika. And I don't want to get stuck in a messy situation where, I will not only loose love as well as a friend."

"Aadvi, you need to understand one thing…love and life are not easy, have never been and never will be…but that does not mean you stop living your life…so why stop loving… carry on with what you have, that is …friendship, who knows your friendship will make inroads to his heart, blossom into something better?"

Aadvi, thought coolly about it for a while and calmed down. She told Avantika about her meeting with Akash on Sunday.

Avantika advised her further, "Aadvi, you need to make the most of this day with him. Don't bottle up these feelings up inside you, show him you have feelings for him, open up."

Aadvi started to think about it from a different perspective now. She decided to take a chance; test the waters. Avantika's words gave her a glimmer of hope. She could see light at the end of the tunnel.

It's risky…but who said love was easy?

After a quiet breakfast the next morning, Rajan and Aadvi left for work. Rajan was sitting in his cabin with his daughter, who was immersed in work, trying her best not to think about Akash or her "date" with him on Sunday. But the restlessness is too much for her to handle; she excused herself and pushed for her cabin to find solitude.

It was 2:30 pm, sitting in her cabin, engrossed in her work. Amidst the silence, the intercom rang. Her secretary informed her about someone's arrival.

"Mam, there is a gentleman here to see you!"

Without giving it a further thought Aadvi asked her to send him inside.

She was stunned to see Akash enter the room with a bunch of Tulips (her favorite flower) she does not exhibit her mixed emotions and politely greeted him.

"Wow, Tulips, how do you know I like these?"

"They were difficult to find but still worth it, knowing they'll cheer you up…I still remember that from our holiday in Keukenhof, you told your Dad you wanted him to buy the Tulip garden."

Aadvi admired the flowers then glancing back at Akash.

"How can I forget that, those were the best times." she paused to admire the Tulips, then looked back at him, "so what brings you by?"

"Well I got off a meeting early today and… wanted to ask you, if you want to grab some lunch? But seems you are loaded with work!" He looked around her cabin.

What do I do, what should I say…darn! The matters of the heart!

"Well you gotta do what you gotta do!"

For one heart stopping moment, their eyes met and Akash couldn't understand his attitude towards her. It was unlike him to ask someone out so easily, even though girls threw themselves at him. He was unsure of what made him so inquisitive towards her.

Maybe we met after so many years, or maybe the fact she's turned our to be so fabulous…whatever it is I am glad to have met her.

Though it was sudden and somewhat awkward since it was not something she had fathomed in the beginning of the day but after pondering over it for a while, she said yes.

"Yeah why not… just let me inform Dad."

"Sure, even I would like to meet him"

They made a move for Rajan's cabin.

"Dad, look who's here to see you?"

Akash entered the cabin.

"Hello uncle, how are you?"

"Oh hello Akash, I am fine, come have a seat, join us for lunch. I was about to call for some Thai food"

"Thank you uncle but I wanted to take Aadvi out for lunch with your permission."

"What's there to ask permission for, go ahead kids, enjoy yourself, Aadvi are you taking your car?"

"I'll drop her back uncle, don't worry." Akash assured him.

"Well alright then, Aadvi, I'll ask the chauffeur to drive your car back home. You kids enjoy your lunch."

She hugged her father as they took leave and headed for his Jaguar Coupe.

Once settled in the car, Aadvi was a bit relieved as well as hopeful.

"So which cuisine would you prefer?" He asked her.

"Italian…my Dad's more of a Thai food fan!"

"Alright Italian it is…how about La Piazza at the Hyatt, it's the best in Delhi, for Italian food!"

"Yeah…I know, been there a couple of times!"

At the restaurant, Akash being a through gentleman treated Aadvi in the manner a lady must be treated and to top it all good wine, great food.

Aadvi was in seventh heaven, her happiness marred by the fact that he was already committed and she couldn't relish this feeling of being pampered knowing it will end all too soon.

"Akash, please don't do this!"

"Don't do what?"

"Don't be so chivalrous, I may just fall for you", she said with a gloomy look on her face.

"So…is that bad or good, I feel it's good, that you will fall for me, at least you'll forever be this sweet to me like you've been since last night."

"Ah, so you are trying to buy my feelings for you? That's cheeky!"

Akash grinned, "that came out all wrong…let me try that again…what I meant was, meeting an old childhood friend after a gazillion years, makes you want to know more about that person."

"We've spent some great times as kids Aadvi, too bad I had to leave else I wouldn't have left a great friend like you. Plus I take great care of the women in my life."

At least there's a start…I do hold a place in his life, he still has a soft spot for me, maybe we do have a chance.

Aadvi had a thoughtful expression of her face as if trying to remember something.

"Hey, what happened to you?" Akash asked inquisitively.

"Nothing, just reminiscing those days, I still remember those holidays, those birthday parties, shopping sprees with our mothers. Their days at the spa, were our days in the pool or at the zoo."

"Tell me what did you do all those years I wasn't around?"

"Nothing much, after you left I concentrated on my studies, traveled around with Dad, joined him at the office and have been with him ever since. What about you?"

"As you know Dad got a huge contract in Mumbai and that was the reason we relocated. It's difficult moving to a new place and starting a new life, but I settled in well, finished my higher secondary from Mumbai and then moved to U.S.

for my studies, came back two years ago and now a full time employee for my Dad at home and office."

"Full time employee?"

"I consider myself his employee. I love my parents a lot, they have given the best they could and most importantly they've given me life, which no amount of money can buy. Their wish is my command, I am my father's full time *sevak*."

She looked at him in admiration and awe.

They finished their lunch and drove around for a while and then proceeded towards her home. It was 6:30 pm, when they reached home and she invited him inside politely.

"Alright now come on, let's us have a cup of tea?"

"No, thank you, but I have to head back, we'll see each other tomorrow."

"Yes we are but my parents will not like you going back like this without even meeting them, come on." She insisted.

The driver handled Akash's car, as they moved towards the entrance of the house. As they entered, Preeti was in the living room, attending some women from a charity she supported.

"Mom, look who is here?"

"Akash, how are you son?" she excused herself from the gathering and moved towards them.

"Very well aunty thought I'd drop Aadvi back and meet you guys."

"That's good, Aadvi take Akash to you Dad. He is in the lounge, I'll join you all, in a while."

Aadvi and Akash walked towards the lounge, where Rajan was sitting dressed casually; smoking a Stradivarius Cigar and watching India take on New Zealand in a 20-20 match at Westpac Stadium.

"Hello uncle, what's the score?" Akash announced his arrival like a true cricket fan.

Rajan looked back, Akash and Aadvi stood at the lounge entrance.

"Oh hello son, not good... another 20 required off the last over and only last wicket in hand!"

"Too bad, I thought Yuvraj made a comeback today and I was hoping he will take the onus upon himself as it is a do or die situation for him."

"It's a team game son...anyway Yuvraj did make 55, but what were the other 10 players doing?"

"Men and their cricket talks...please excuse me."

Aadvi pushed off to her room to freshen up. The last wicket fell and it was curtains down for India in the 3 match series, which New Zealand won 2-1.

"Anyway it's over…" he switched off the T.V. "so tell me how was lunch?"

"It was fun. I am glad we could catch up on old times and all those times that we were not around for each other. We had so much to share. She's a superb girl and a great friend."

"Well, she's an even greater daughter." Preeti declared as she entered the lounge.

"Akash, have a seat, come share a drink with me, what will you have?" Rajan insisted.

"Sure uncle, but I'll prefer coffee. Have to drive back home soon as some old school buddies are coming over."

"So boys night huh…" Rajan prodded him.

"Yeah uncle, but we are just going to catch up…play video games…the usual"

The butler was asked to fetch coffee. Preeti moved to the kitchen to monitor arrangements for dinner; Akash took a seat on the couch next to Rajan.

"So Akash, how is work and how are finding the work culture of Delhi as compared to Mumbai?"

"The difference is huge uncle, although the work is fine, the only difference is the pace at which things are done here. Mumbai is fast paced while Delhi still has the traditional mindset. Doing things at their own pace, irrespective of the fact that it could cause loss to the other person."

"I agree with you. But times change, let's hope for a better future."

The butler arrived with coffee and Preeti persisted Akash to stay for dinner.

"Akash, why don't you stay back for dinner?"

"I would love to aunty but I have to head back." quickly sipping his coffee.

Aadvi entered the room, looking fresher and holding a box.

"What's that darling?" Rajan asked her.

"This is my box of memories, Dad."

She opened the box to reveal her keepsakes and old photos. It had pictures of her parent's wedding, pictures of her maternal and paternal grandparents, her friends, school trips, from her birthday parties, her holidays, some of which had Akash and his family holidaying with them… Holland, Disneyland in Orlando, Skiing trips to Swiss Alps.

Ah…those were the days!

Akash was hit by nostalgia and looked at Aadvi; he couldn't help notice the way she was admiring his photos. He got hold of a photo, which had Aadvi and Akash making a sandcastle together.

"Hey Aadvi"

"Yeah"

"Can I please keep this photo for myself?"

"Yes sure." she smiled back at him.

"Uncle, aunty, I'll take leave now…Aadvi, I'll pick you sharp at 11:00…be ready." he says getting up from the sofa.

All of them headed to the entrance of the house and the driver fetched Akash's car. Akash touched Rajan and Preeti's feet and made a move for his car. Aadvi stood there waving him goodbye with a lovesick look on her face. She just couldn't wipe off the grin. The wait for the next day made her all the more anxious.

Questions baffled her mind!

CHAPTER 4

Nothing much was discussed over the dinner table except that, Rajan conveyed Aadvi about a piece of news much to her shock and delight.

"Aadvi…myself and Inderjeet are coming over to the club at well for some golf and I will talk to Inder about you guys, see what his reaction is and God willing if he says yes, *Naanu* will go to his house to officially ask Inder and Roma for their consent." he is silent for a while, "from your reaction last night we could make out that you liked him, that's the reason for me to push this case. He is a great guy and his parents adore you. So don't lose hope, even if he likes an American girl, I know Inder will never agree."

Hrajn was adamant about talking to Inderjeet, which gave Aadvi a sense of contentment. She finished her dinner and bid goodnight to her parents.

While heading towards her room, the thought of how unpredictable life can be and what had just happened hit her…in the morning, she didn't want to think about him let alone going for lunch date with him and now the idea of getting married to the man she was enamoured with, made her even more restless.

She dragged her tired body to the bed, thinking about what is and what could be. A sense of optimism overtook her.

Even if he does propose, Andrea could reject his proposal. We like each other; he might was well accept the proposal Dad sends his way.
Only time will tell.

The next morning Aadvi was all smiles, opening the windows, letting in the light breeze as it rumpled her hair across her flawless face…it was not one of those usual mornings, it seemed different…she seemed different.

Aadvi joined Preeti and Rajan at the dining table for a late breakfast. Looking every bit the golfer in a baby pink golfing tee and white golfing pants and shoes. She helped herself to a bowl of cereal.

"All set, dear?"

"Yes Mom."

Her heart thumped, as she stared at the clock.
Tick tock, tick tock, tick tock…the antique grandfather clock teased her.

Dong, dong, dong…it was 11

Aadvi tried rushed her cereal.

"Eat slowly dear."

"Mom, he could be here any minute!"

She was about to finish, when her phone rang. It was Akash.

"Hello, Good Morning Akash."

"Hey Good Morning, I am about to reach your place… Hope you're ready?"

"You bet I am!"

The cupid's arrow had struck her hard and how she hoped the cherub would one-day work it's magic on him too.

Is it love, am I falling truly, madly and deeply in love with him?

She rushed towards the gate as the butler carried her Mizuno clubs to the car.

Akash, waited outside the parked Panamera, opened the door for her. Dressed in black golf tee and khaki colored golf pants and shoes…looking quiet the stud.

Hmm…I could so get used to him.

She took the seat next to him as they exited the gate…the car raced away towards the golf club.

"So, how are you doing this morning?"

"Great…it's a nice day for golf…it was a good idea."

"Dad told me him and uncle are also joining us today, but they will join us a little late."

"We can brush up on skills in the meantime…haha"

Driving at a fast pace, they reached the club soon and Akash helped her get her bag of clubs out of the car. They moved towards the driving range.

"I am quiet rusty?" he declared as he walked towards the driving range.

"Not as rusty as I am…I love golf, but hardly get chance to take some time out for it."

Akash settled his Callaway clubs at the driving range, as they prepared to tee off. He took out his driver and launched one about 210 yards, and she tried to do her best by firing one about 190 yards.

They carried on playing for an hour and a half. With the sun burning, they decided to take a break and moved their golf cart towards the restaurant.

They got seated and ordered a pitcher of lemonade.

"Aadvi, I am so glad we met after so many years. It's easy to find good friends but I found mine to the greatest."

Aadvi has an ecstatic look on her face. She was glad to have him by her side. These moments were precious for her.

"Thank you so much for the kind words Akash. You've been such a gentleman as well."

They looked at each other, albeit with different thoughts. Akash saw only a good friend in her although Aadvi hoped for a future with him.

Just then Rajan and Inderjeet walked in.

"Hello kids!" Inderjeet called out.

"Hi uncle." Aadvi acknowledged his presence.

"Hey Dad, hello uncle." Akash was glad to see them.

"Why aren't you at the golf course?" Rajan asked Aadvi.

"We played for about an hour and a half and decided to take a breather as it grew hotter."

"The summers have been blazing hot this year!" Rajan pulled a chair.

"Dad where are your clubs?" Akash inquired.

"We decided against playing in these conditions, we'll grab a beer or two and join you guys later."

"Sorry Dad, I wouldn't want Aadvi or me to get a sunburn, we'd better utilize our time at a cooler place. I want to catch a movie, but first we'll have some lunch … what say Aadvi?"

"Sure, why not?"

Aadvi was elated. Rajan too, was delighted to see his daughter happy and Akash taking such care of her.

"Inder, let the kids go, I want to talk to you alone."

"Alright you kids go enjoy yourselves. We'll join you at home, Rajan uncle and Preeti aunty and Aadvi are joining us for dinner tonight."

"Hey that's great Dad. Come on Aadvi, let's leave, got to pick up tickets as well."

Akash and Aadvi bid them adieu and moved towards the exit as Rajan ordered beer for himself and Inderjeet.

"Rajan, now tell me, what was so important?"

"Jeet, I wanted to talk to you about Akash and Aadvi."

"What about them?"

"Jeet, I really like your son for my daughter and would like your say on the matter!"

"I am going to stop you right there Rajan!"

Rajan was taken aback at Inderjeet's reaction.

"I know what you're going to say buddy, but I will say it before you do…yes! In fact I wanted to speak to you regarding that myself. Roma likes Aadvi very much and Akash himself has been singing her praises these days. I want your daughter's hand for my son."

"But Jeet listen to me and don't rush into anything, I want you to talk to Akash first. See what he clearly thinks about Aadvi, one can't lay the burden of their decisions or ideas on their kids in today's times and from what Aadvi has told me, Akash likes some American girl back in New York and is pretty serious about her!"

"Rajan, Akash is my son and knows the value of my promise, he knows whatever decision his parents will take, and he'll respect that, you don't worry and trust me, Aadvi is going to be my daughter-in-law."

He continued to be assertive, "Rajan, Akash is my son and I guarantee that he'll do as I say."

"So Papa, Aadvi's *Naanu*, will officially come for a small ceremony, is that ok with you?"

"*Jee aya nu*…bring Papa along with you tonight and we'll have a small ceremony as home and then a bigger function in a few days time."

"No not today as he is not well, let us give him some time to recover as he's the elder of the family."

"Ok no problem, now let's toast to our friendship."

And they raised their glasses, with the hopes of taking their friendship forward to a new level.

In the meantime, Akash and Aadvi reached Set'z at the Emporio having booked the tickets earlier from the app on his phone.

The hostess seated them as the server handed them the menus.

"So what are your plans Akash…workwise…do you plan to start something on your own soon or prefer working for uncle?"

"Well, Dad has a project in the pipeline and he wants me to take charge and frankly I want it more than him…he plans to start a hotel project in New York and that also gives me chance to get back to my life, my Andrea."

Aadvi felt her stomach getting queasy and heart racing. She seemed shaken but took the whole thing sportingly. She was still optimistic that things might change and so will his heart and feelings towards her once his parents give their approval for the marriage.

"Oh really, even Dad wants me to head a project in New York in collaboration with a cosmetics company based in Orangeburg. Who knows we might meet in New York soon."

"Oh great, knock on the wood."

"So when are you planning to go back?"

"Once I talk to Dad about Andrea and convince him especially my Mom who has always dreamt of the perfect Indian *bahu*, once they say yes, I'll take the first flight to New York."

His words left a bitter taste in her mouth.

They finished their lunch and headed towards the multiplex to watch the latest offering from Ridley Scott. Though she would've preferred the mini theater constructed by her father at home for the privacy, she went there for Akash.

They left the theater at 6.30 and drove towards Akash's palatial residence in Gurgaon. The car entered the driveway. It was a beautiful house, with a huge garden with cleanly trimmed bushes, perfectly mowed grass and ornate with the most beautiful summer flowers. And to top it all was the enviable line-up of the best luxury cars. The Olympic sized swimming pool at the back didn't hurt either.

They entered the house. The house was very stylishly decked up with Ming vases, handpicked antiques and crystal showpieces from Austria.

"Welcome kids" Roma, welcomed them as she comes out of the kitchen.

"Hello Aunty, how are you?"

"I am fine…so how was your day?"

"It was tiring Mom, but I am glad we could have some time together."

"Well it's great you got some time to catch up…Aadvi, your Dad is with Inderjeet uncle in the billiard room and I am going to join your Mother who is in the living room. Akash, take her and show her around the house."

"Sure thing Mom."

Akash showed her around his palace. A palace he was the sole Prince of since he had no siblings. He took her to his room and showed her his collection of music, a passion they both shared.

"So you want to hear something?"

"Sure play anything you wish!" she says getting comfortable on the lazyboy.

He began strumming an old Hindi song. It was a magical time for Aadvi, not only did he play wonderful music but also had a silky voice. She was mesmerized.

It was well set room especially for guy. He had a fabulous collection of music, ranging from Neil Diamond, Pink Floyd, Metallica, Bruce Springsteen, The Rolling Stones and Elvis to Mukesh, Kishore and Rafi. He was a music lover like her and their choices were almost similar.

He was an out and out gaming freak, as suggested by Xbox and Playstation 4 consoles and the huge stack of video games, piled next to the T.V.

The tour ended with Akash and Aadvi heading for the living room where their mother's discussed their respective household matters.

"Hey kids, what'll you have?" Roma asked them.

Without even letting her speak, Akash cuts in.

"I want coffee mom…what about you Aadvi?"

"Yeah, coffee will do!"

Roma instructed the maid to get coffee, while Preeti and Roma enjoyed red wine and were joined by Inderjeet and Rajan in the living room.

"So kids, how was your day?"

"It was great Dad, how was you game, did you finally get a chance to tee off?"

"Oh no, it was dreadfully hot. We preferred chilled beer to putting under the blistering sun. Came back home a few hours ago and have been playing billiards ever since. Thanks to you two, I got a chance to spend time with my best friend."

"And thanks to you, I got to spend time with mine." Akash smiled at her.

The butler informed them about the dinner being ready. They moved towards the dining room.

A typically lavish Punjabi food prepared in homemade *desi ghee* awaited them on an impeccably set table.

While everyone else gorged on the butter chicken and the *dal makhani,* Akash stuck to salad and grilled chicken.

No wonder he looks so trimmed!

The dinner finished and *Kesari Kheer* a specialty of Khanna household was served as dessert.

The Kapoor's took leave and made their way towards their car. Rajan and Preeti took their seats and Aadvi, just about to enter the car, paused…she just couldn't resist looking back over her shoulder; she looked hard at him, as if trying to convey something. He looked right back at her, trying to figure why she suddenly stopped.

Their eyes met again…questions still unanswered.

CHAPTER 5

Back at the Kapoor house; 12:15 am, Rajan got a frantic call.

"Hello, Rajan Sir, this is Joginder this side!"

"Yes Joginder, what happened, why are you calling at this hour, is everything ok?"

"No Sir, Mr.Chopra is not feeling well and wants you all here…please Sir, leave of the estate, as soon as possible."

"Don't worry Joginder, we'll leave right away."

Aadvi was informed about her *Naanu* on the intercom and they left for the estate. In the meantime, Joginder informed Dr.Verma who had been Mr.Chopra's cardiologist for the last few years.

In Mr. Chopra's room, Aadvi, Rajan and Preeti were at his bedside as he stared at the photo gifted by Aadvi on his birthday, hanging on the wall in front of his bed as Dr.Verma examined him.

"Mr.Kapoor, we have to move him to a hospital right away."

"But what seems to be the problem?"

"His breathing is not normal and pulse rate is fluctuating. He'll be well taken care off in a hospital than here…it's just for precaution"

"Take whatever action you need doctor."

An ambulance was arranged and Mr.Chopra was rushed to the nearest multi-speciality hospital.

He was put on oxygen concentrator for the night while being constantly monitored. Since only one attendant was allowed to stay in the room, Rajan decided to spend the night in the hospital while Aadvi along with her mother were sent home.

The next morning Akash called Aadvi, but was shocked to hear the news about her *Naanu*. He informed his parents and they rushed to see Mr.Chopra. Aadvi and Preeti joined Rajan at the hospital. Mr.Chopra was asleep.

"Hope he wasn't restless?" Preeti asked wiping her tears.

"Yes he did, he slept peacefully, don't worry dear, he'll be fine."

Aadvi comforted her mother.

Akash arrived with his parents. Aadvi was pleased to see how thoughtful Akash and his parents were and greeted them.

With the room crowding up, they moved towards the waiting area, where they were constantly in touch with Rajan who was still in the room in discussion with the doctor.

The doctor inspected Mr.Chopra and appeared to be happy with his improvement. But insisted he stayed for one more day, but Mr.Chopra's refused, as he wanted to go home. He requested the doctor to discharge him as soon as possible.

"Dr.Verma, I want to go back home, I can't stay here for one more night."

"But Mr.Chopra, you'll be well taken care off here than at home!"

"I understand that but, my family is enough to take care of me."

After pondering over it for a while, the doctor relented and asked his assistant to have Mr.Chopra's discharge papers ready.

Rajan's secretary Ashok who joined him at the hospital got the papers ready and settled the bill. They were set to leave for the Chopra estate where Joginder, had made all the necessary arrangements for his master as per the instructions of Dr.Verma.

An oxygen concentrator was in place and a male nurse had been arranged for him full-time.

They reached home and Mr. Chopra was settled on his bed. He looked at everyone around him. Inderjeet and his family were also present, which made Mr. Chopra even more content. And seeing Akash standing next to Aadvi, his happiness knew no bounds.

Mr.Chopra saw Inderjeet standing next to Rajan; he called him, closer to his bedside.

"Inder, *puttar*, I want to talk to you about something."

"Yes, please go ahead Uncle."

"I want to ask your son's hand in marriage for my Aadvi."

Akash was flabbergasted. He couldn't believe what he'd heard.

"I promise you…Akash will marry Aadvi…we will get them married as soon as possible."

For Aadvi, it seemed like a cocktail of emotions, the grief of seeing her grandfather in such state was saddening while the thought of getting married to man she loved was moment of pure elation.

Akash on the other hand felt traumatized by what was going on… as though his whole world came crashing in that one moment, his dreams of having a future with Andrea seemed long gone and he was helpless.

"This is what I was hoping to hear, God Bless you son, this is what I had hoped for…to see my…" he began to stutter.

With Mr. Chopra's condition worsening with every passing second and his breathing subsiding, Dr.Verma got called right away. But the strong palpitations took control. In a few moments, the inevitable happened as Aadvi's beloved *Naanu* left for his heavenly abode.

Their pillar of strength had fallen.

Preeti was devastated; hugging her father's body while Rajan sat on a chair, head buried in his hands, trying to absorb what had just happened. Mr.Chopra had been a guiding light for him after his father's demise.

Aadvi being in utter state of shock leaned against the wall.

Roma consoled Aadvi and Preeti while Inderjeet and Akash looked after Rajan.

The preparations of the funeral procession and cremation were done. Family and friends, who a short time ago had gathered to celebrate his 75th birthday, were all present bidding final goodbye to the great man. The who's who of the city and the business world attended the funeral at Lodhi Ghat.

A few days after Mr.Chopra's demise, Aadvi and her mother were still trying to cope with the sorrow.

The talks about the wedding also lay low for while, Akash was at ease too, thinking it'll pass and he'll be out of it soon. Nonetheless he tried his best to talk his father completely out of it on the pretext of Aadvi still grieving her *Naanu's* death but his voice fell on deaf ears, as his father was stubborn man.

And one day, Inderjeet finally decided to take things ahead and to talk to Rajan on the situation. They met over drinks one evening.

"Rajan, I think we should proceed with the wedding arrangement!"

"But Inder, isn't it too soon?"

"Rajan, don't forget it was Mr.Chopra's last wish and I made a promise to him. Besides, it'll do a world of good to both families. Preeti will immerse herself in the wedding preparations and Aadvi will find her happiness with Akash."

Rajan was still unsure whether it's right to talk about the wedding so soon with Preeti who was still mourning the loss of her father, but nonetheless he did, considering it was Mr.Chopra's last wish.

"Preeti…as Papa desired do you want me to go ahead with the wedding?"

Preeti had immense pain and tears in her eyes.

"Yes…although his presence will be sorely missed but this is what he wanted…it was his last wish."

"Alright, I'll talk to Inder."

In the evening, Rajan went to Inderjeet's house.

They were seated in the home office and discussing over coffee on how to go about the situation.

"Inder, have you had a chance to speak to Akash about Aadvi?"

"No, not yet, but don't worry…he's my son and he knows the value of my promise. He will agree to whatever decision his parents will take for him and where Aadvi is concerned, he will never refuse since he likes her very much."

As the two friends were engrossed in the conversation, Akash walked in with some official files in hand.

"Hello uncle, how are you and how are aunty and Aadvi doing now?"

Akash hadn't spoken to Aadvi in a while, since she was not in the right frame of mind. Inderjeet was stunned on Aaksh's question as he was the one who seemed to be in touch with Aadvi and had been pestering him to delay all the talks.

"They both are better now…trying to cope with the loss."

Akash could make out as to why Rajan was there. He showed the files to his father and walked out of the room hurriedly so as to avoid any awkward talk related the to the "wedding."

Rajan was still skeptical about the timing but Inderjeet assured Rajan again that there was nothing to worry about.

As soon as Rajan left, Inderjeet called Akash to his room.

The moment he had been dreading was here.

Akash entered the room, where his father sat on the couch, smoking a cigarette.

"Dad, you called me?"

"Yes son, come have a seat!"

Akash sat next to his father with his heart pounding.

"Son, as you know Rajan's father-in-law took a promise from me and the fact is, me and your Mother also like Aadvi a lot... and we want to see you settle down soon. What I expect of you is simple; we want you to get married to Aadvi. She is nice girl, you like her a lot and as far as I know she likes you too."

"Dad...Aadvi is a great girl no doubt about that, but I've always seen her as a friend and nothing more...I am in love with someone else."

"Well...who is she?" Inderjeet didn't want to give away, that he knew about her through Rajan.

For Akash it was now or never. He had to divulge the details.

"Dad her name is Andrea...Andrea Johnson, she lives in New York and works as a model, I met her at a fashion show a few years ago...I know this'll be hard but please tell uncle to stop pursuing this further."

"Akash I never expected this of you...you are asking me to turn my back on a promise I made to my friend!"

"And what are you doing Dad? Asking me to turn my back on my love!"

There was a dreadful silence in the room. Roma walked in having listend to everything at the door.

"Raj...apologise to your father and I am you mother and I expect you to do what I say!"

"Mom, I will apologise to Dad...but you can't force me to marry Aadvi!"

"Akash what is the guarantee that the girl of your choice is the right one for our family?"

Akash was silent.

"Aadvi is a superb girl, we like her you like her, even I know she likes you...she'll be the perfect life partner for you." Roma was persistent.

"Mom, Dad, I will explain everything to Aadvi and I know the kind of girl she is ...she will understand my situation. Anyway you can't be more wrong about Aadvi being interested in me, I told her about Andrea when we met at the party the other night" his tone now increasingly louder, "and she was quiet supportive of us, unlike you."

"Don't you dare speak to me in that tone, young man." Inderjeet warned him.

"I am sorry Dad, but I can't go through with this!"

"And we are also not going through with whatever you are saying…I can't accept a ramp model in skimpy clothes to be my daughter-in-law."

"Dad I will make sure she quits and besides she's a model not a stripper." Akash accepted a responsibility even he wasn't sure off, but anything to get this situation off his back.

"I am ashamed of you Aakash!" Roma was saddened by whatever had happened.

"Well you have put me a spot of bother with my friend, how am I supposed to say no to him now…they are eagerly awaiting an affirmative response from us."

"Don't worry, I'll speak to Aadvi, she's smart enough to make her parents understand…I trust her."

"Whatever you do, just think about it twice…Aadvi is a great girl!"

"I'll handle it!" Akash left the room and headed outside to call Aadvi on her mobile.

"Hello Aadvi, how are you holding up now?"

"I am fine but Mom is still in shock."

"Aadvi, please convey my condolences to aunty tell her to stay strong."

"Yeah thanks, I'll do that."

"Aadvi, is it possible to meet you today, need to discuss a few things with you."

"Yeah sure…but what's the problem, you seem stressed?"

"No, everything's fine, just need to let out something."

"OK where should I meet you?"

"No problem, I'll pick you in the next 30 minutes."

"Alright, I'll wait for you."

Aadvi was perplexed. Her mind was on a roller coaster of emotions; butterflies in her stomach.

What happened? Why does he need to meet me all of a sudden?

She informed her mother about the call. Even Preeti failed to understand why Akash would want to meet Aadvi all of a sudden that too when her father was there a few hours ago discussing their marriage.

Akash arrived on time. He didn't want to lose another minute before situation went out of control.

Aadvi took a seat while Akash drove at fast pace, sitting quietly. His expressions and silence were just too much to handle.

They reached a nearby hotel and head for the café.

"What happened Akash, hope everything is fine?" she asked in a nervous tone as she took a seat.

"Aadvi, I am sorry I had to meet you like this but whatever has been happening over the last few days is just too much for me to handle."

"Why what happened?"

"You very well know your *Naanu*…God Bless his soul, took a promise from my father that our parents get us married and my father made that commitment. And even your father supported the idea."

Aadvi gulped a glass of water, listening to him.

"And to top it all they've come up with a crazy theory that you love me…"

Aadvi stared at him; her ears awaited the bad news.

"Aadvi, I can't take the pressure anymore…you know I love someone else and even if we did get married, none of us would ever be happy knowing that the marriage has no meaning."

Aadvi glanced at him, controlling the flood of tears in her eyes.

"I am asking this as a friend…will you please help me put an end to this charade?"

Charade…he thinks this is all a charade…his father's promise, my love for him…a charade!

Tears stung the eyes, but she managed to fight them back.

Akash hung his head low, between his palms.

Aadvi decided to get it over with this time, not willing to spend a second more in the company of such a callous person.

"Akash, I have forever been a friend to you and I am very proud of you for being so honest about the whole thing. …But you are wrong that I like you…I do not like you…"

He looked up.

"I love you."

"Sorry…loved you, but not anymore, the last few days were like an illusion and now the time is up, so is the illusion…"
"When you came back and I saw you at the party that night, something just happened to me, in that one awesome and captivating moment I lost my heart to you. But it doesn't mean that I am a man stealer, you love Andrea…you go get her, true love is unconditional and I never set any conditions for you to stay in a relationship where your heart isn't."

"But what about our parents, they'll never understand!"

"You don't worry about it, I'll handle that. Now I request you to please drop me back"

She just wanted to get out of there as fast as she could… it was getting difficult to fight back the tears.

Akash was silent…out of words to say to this very dear friend of whom, he sung praises of, day and night, with whom he spent some great moments of his childhood… whom he had unwillingly hurt.

He dropped her home; no goodbyes shared between them.

Aadvi ran inside and he couldn't do anything to comfort her.

He reached home to find another situation. Akash entered his father's room and found his father lying on the bed, unwell, still reeling from the effects of his son's decision, and his mother turned away, not even willing to even look at him.

All because of me…what have I done…Dad is unwell, Mom isn't speaking to me, Aadvi is sad because of me…but what can I do? I love Andrea!

He took his father's hand in his own, tears of emotion and guilt ran from his eyes. His father opened his eyes and witnessesed his grown up son in a pitiful state and tears flowed from his eyes too. Father and son shared glances. He couldn't face his father in that state anymore and left the room.

Back in the Kapoor mansion, Aadvi was miserable, as Preeti and Rajan entered her room. Rajan understood what had been bothering his daughter. He recalled how she had warned them about Akash being in love with someone else.

"You don't need to say anything Princess...I understand and I am sorry my actions have caused you so much heartache." Rajan felt guilty, knowing Aadvi had warned him of such a situation.

Preeti hugged her daughter tightly and tried to calm her down. Aadvi stopped crying after a while and fell asleep. Preeti gave her a blanket, switched off the light and exited the room.

The next morning, Aadvi was in a calmer frame of mind and even joined her parents at the breakfast table. Rajan and Preeti were happy to see their daughter easing up.

Rajan's mobile rang and he was informed about Inderjeet's health. They rushed to see him. Aadvi entered the room and met Roma. Inderjeet, who was being attended by his doctor, saw Aadvi standing next to Roma, tears of remorse filled his eyes. He asked Aadvi to sit beside him.

As Aadvi took a seat next to him, Inderjeet, like a father placed his hand on her head, thinking what an idiot his son is, to have given up on a great girl like her and lamented his luck as he lost out on a great daughter-in-law.

"Aadvi, dear, I am sorry." as he folded both his hands apologizing.

"No uncle, you don't have to be apologetic for anything... when it's not meant to be it's not meant to be."

"God Bless you my child. It's his loss, that he can't see what a gem you are while he's running after a mere pebble."

"Who know's uncle, Andrea might be a good choice for him...just give them a chance."

The Kapoor's stayed a while and then took leave so that Inderjeet could rest.

As they headed towards the stairs, Akash crossed Aadvi's path, coming out from his room.

They looked at each other.

He didn't have any words to say to her but tried nevertheless. Rajan and Preeti left them alone and went downstairs. Aadvi conveyed him the news he was hoping for...that her parents had taken the proposal off the table.

"Thank you Aadvi...thank you so much, you've been an angel, I am sure Andrea will appreciate it more than me once she knows what you've done for us. Another thing...I hope you won't refuse."

"What now?" She couldn't stand him anymore.

"Aadvi you deserve so much better in life...maybe I am not worthy of your love. Still I hope you will not refuse me what I am going to ask you for..."

"What is it?"

"Please move on…find someone…get married…or else I won't be able to forgive myself ever or face your parents who are very dear to me."

Aadvi could only fake a nod. He extended his hand.

"Goodbye Aadvi!"

"Goodbye Akash!"

They shook hands and parted ways. She turned and she moved down the stairs, where her parents awaited her. Taking a seat beside her mother with tear filled eyes; heart drowning in a tidal wave of emotions, she left the premises of the house, hoping never to come back there. A guilt ridden Aaksh stood in the balcony hoping Aadvi would move on and he will be free of the burden.

CHAPTER 6

A month had passed since her heart broke, Aadvi was trying hard to get back to her normal routine. There was no contact between her and Akash anymore; she didn't even know what happened between him and Andrea. Even her parents lost touch with Akash's parents, as they felt humiliated by their son's actions. Rajan and Preeti tried their best to cheer up and look for potential suitors for their daughter.

But Aadvi was not ready.

One day she politely asked her father, who was sitting in the office.

"Dad, I want to speak to you!"

"Yes Princess, tell me, what is it?"

"Dad, I want to go away for a while."

"That's a good idea, let's plan a holiday, where do you want to go?"

"Dad, what I meant was away from, Delhi, away from everyone and everything. I just need some time out."

"Aadvi, if you want to go, I will not stop you. Go out there for the right reasons. Escaping from your problems is not the answer…Why don't you go to New York, stay at the Penthouse, try and relax for sometime, and if you want you can start working at our New York office or even start working on that cosmetics project you were so keen on!"

"Thanks Dad, I'd really appreciate that."

"Don't worry, I'll make the necessary arrangements."

Father and daughter shared a tight hug. And Aadvi left the room with a content look.

All the arrangements were made and Preeti while not in favor of sending Aadvi away from herself gave her approval only for the sake of her daughter's happiness and to save her sanity.

Aadvi left for New York. After a tedious flight, she reached JFK at 10 pm, headed towards the exit where the company limo was in place to pick her up and take her to their Penthouse on the Upper East Side. Her father bought the handsome Penthouse a few years ago. It was modern, very chic, living room wide enough to hold a party, three bedrooms and a separate dining room; the kitchen was fully equipped, a bar to entertain guests, while the balcony gave a spectacular view of the city's skyline.

Aadvi reached the place, had a look around admiring her Dad's sense of investment. She called to inform her father that she had reached the safely.

"Hey Dad!"

"Hello dear, hope you reached safe and sound?"

"Yes Dad I just reached the Penthouse, it's almost 11:30, just going to take some rest now."

"Alright dear, goodnight and call me if you need anything!"

"Sure Dad, goodnight!" she hangs up.

Arching her back, she lay down on the couch, closed her eyes and took a deep breath. Her new life beckoned her.

The morning, Aadvi woke up fresher, something she hadn't done in weeks; new places, new faces and a new life awaited her. After a quick shower, she unpacked and went for some grocery shopping to a nearby grocery store.

She reserved the evening for some much needed recreation. She poured herself a glass of Shiraz and grabbed a book. She wanted to be completely relaxed for work the next day.

It was a bright sunny New York morning, Aadvi was happy; at least she was trying to be. Relishing every bit of the solitude she got. She was through with her bath, got dressed and whipped up some breakfast. Dressed in a white shirt and beige business suit with pearl earrings to go with it; she was ready for her new beginning.

The car was ready and so was she.

She had been to New York twice before but never looked at the city like today. This was her city now, she was one of them, the hot dog stands, the florists on the sidewalk, the café's and the food joints, the richness of cultures, the people, she was in love with the city instantly.

With the lyrics of New York, New York, constantly running in her mind.

If I can make it there,
I'll make it anywhere.
It's up to you, New York, New York.

Aadvi reached the office situated at Lexington Avenue in Manhattan. A short drive from the Penthouse, her father opened the office to overlook their overseas projects. Aadvi too, was interested in starting a new venture with a cosmetic company based in Orangeburg.

The manager of the office who was of south Indian decent welcomed her. Mr. Ramakrishnan Kutty or Kutty as most people fondly called him, came to New York 5 years ago. Hired by Rajan himself, who recruited him from a debate on "changing face of telecom industry" where Rajan was the chief guest. He could see the spark in the young lad and offered him a job after finishing his studies.

A young chap all of 27 but married with two kids. He was tall, dusky as well as husky with a great sense of humor. He even started a weekly, half hour one man show, just for fun, which he performed live on Friday evenings for the whole staff, aptly titled, "Everybody loves Kutty."

It was 10:15 am. Aadvi settled in her cabin, soaking in the drastic change in her life, just as Kutty knocked on her door.

"May I come in mam?"

"Yes Mr. Kutty, please do come in."

"Please mam, call me Kutty, everyone here does."

"Alight Kutty, then you make it a point to tell everyone here to call me Aadvi and not mam."

"Sure Aadvi. Here are some papers, which Rajan Sir, asked me to show you as soon as you reached the office, please have a look. I'll collect these later."

"Sure Kutty, I'll go through these, in the meantime could you please have the performance record of the employees from the last quarter, sent to me."

"Sure Aadvi, I'll send it to you right away."

Kutty left the cabin.

Aadvi looked around her cabin, which was decorated quiet well. It was a bright room, with a huge window, giving a perfect view of the skyline of the world's most loved city. The walls adorned by the pictures of her father, two of them with the mayor of New York, one with the President himself from a charity dinner a few years ago. The benevolent guy that Rajan was, he supported a number of charities, big and small.

Dad...I am missing you too much, wish you were here!

But bigger things were at stake here, her father's trust in her and her determination to get over a "certain" chapter of her life.

A few months passed and Aadvi immersed herself in work. Living alone in a huge place made her more lonesome, she bought a French bulldog to keep her company. And since the building was pet friendly, she decided to give it a try. Though she had never kept a pet before, but they both adjusted well with each other. She named him Amigo.

Her cousins visited her for a couple of days. She was in constant touch with Avantika who was now married and settled in Australia. Avantika planned a holiday in the Big Apple once her husband's official leave was approved. Aadvi looked forward to meeting her since she couldn't be at the wedding as it took place the week her grandfather died.

And the circumstances related to Akash and his family prompted her to come to New York so hurriedly that she couldn't even meet her best friend.

But that was in the past...the present was exciting and the future looked bright. She even struck the deal with the cosmetic company in Orangeburg. She was going to start a new division, on her own.

Life was looking better…but not for long.

A charity, supported by her father amongst the other millionaires of the city for the homeless, was organizing a dinner with Sean Whitman as the chief guest.

The name seemed to ring a bell, but she wasn't quiet sure. Aadvi, asked Kutty about Sean as the invitation stated his name. Kutty told her about him and Aadvi seemed less than impressed. Now she recalled the name, which she had read many at times in the tabloids.

Sean Whitman…young, dashing, a Harvard graduate and sole heir to the billions of textile and media giant, Shane Whitman. Shane was now separated from Donna, his wife of 30 years. They separated when Sean was 7 years old. He was now seeing a young socialite and wannabe actress Cheryl Wood, 20 years younger than him and a blonde, whose only claim to fame was her Playboy cover shot.

All of 28, Sean was actively involved in numerous charity projects and even traveled with the American Red Cross Society for special missions to Africa as a volunteer. A passionate painter, and a good one at that, he raised millions for the organizations involved in providing shelter to the homeless.

But his playboy lifestyle kept him mostly in the news than the charitable nature. He was notorious for being in company of sexy women most of the time. A new model every month for a girlfriend or just arm candy.

Though she didn't want to go at first since the event was on a Saturday night and her work hardly gave her any time for relaxation or Amigo, but after much persuasion by her father over the phone, she relented and decided to go. Since she was supposed to drop a cheque for donation as well, that made her presence all the more important.

Aadvi asked her secretary Nora, to confirm the organizers of her presence for the event.

And Saturday evening came soon. Amigo was acting crazy… he just wouldn't let her go. He made his displease evident to Aadvi, by hiding the one shoe from pair of golden pumps she had selected earlier in the evening. He played hardball but Aadvi eventually found it tucked in his bed.

She reached the event being held at Park Avenue South sharp at 7. Dressed in a lovely Alberta Ferretti black evening gown with brushed with gold, matched with black diamond stud earrings and golden Jimmy Choo pumps. She looked sizzling and heads turned. The stunning Ms. Kapoor was a new addition to the crème de la crème of New York.

The cheques were collected at the reception area of the hall. Aadvi dropped her $ 500,000 cheque and proceeded towards the hall. Her seat was very close to the stage and to keep up with the boring speeches was tedious. Aadvi found solace in the wine and the hors d'oeuvre's were delectable enough to keep her attentive.

The man of the hour, the one everyone had been waiting for had arrived. Sean Whitman was there and had the females going gaga over him. He looked elegant, suave, stood tall at 6 feet, broad shoulders, dressed in a black, suit with a bow tie sporting a quiff on light brown hair, grey eyes, clean shaven face oozing machismo. There was something about him that made him stand out in the crowd.

Not bad!

Sean walked up to the dais to a round of applause.

Aadvi was inquisitive from the moment he started speaking.

"Friends, we've gathered for great cause this evening. After United States and with your continuous support, the home sweet home project has taken off well in Africa. And I am glad to announce the commencement of the project to build 150 homes for the people of the cities of Bungo, Cabamba, Luena, Huambo and Malanje in Angola thereafter there are 5 more projects in the pipeline meant to target one country after the other as per their needs and assistance available from generous supporters like yourself. I am also announcing a personal donation of $ 2 million from Whitman Incorporated"

"So without taking further time, I would like to congratulate each one of you who has been a part of this great project and request you all to applaud yourselves."

He left the dais, to a standing ovation. As luck would have it, amongst the sea of faces applauding and cheering him, his eyes fell on Aadvi who looked right back at him, still admiring him, although only for his benevolence, Kutty's description of his playboy ways still stuck in her mind.

Why is he smiling at me, should I smile back? Hope the playboy doesn't get any wrong ideas!

After the speeches hold off, the cocktails were in full flow and dinner was served. Aadvi was alone, no one knew her and vice versa. To fight off the boredom, she headed to the bar to get herself another glass of wine, when Whitman Jr. came to her rescue.

"Hello there…Sean Whitman!" a manly and sensual voice called out extending his hand, a glass of scotch in the other.

"Hello…Aadvi Kapoor"

He looked even more striking on a closer look, than on stage. Her exquisiteness too, captivated him.

"Aadvi…you seem to be new here…not one of the regulars, I mean I've never seen you around at the charity dinner, though it's a quarterly event!"

"Well you are right, I am actually filling in for my father, Mr.Rajan Kapoor."

"Oh yes, I know him very well, the telecom king from India."

"Well I can't say whether he's a king or not financially, but he's a king to me."

"Why…what makes you think that?"

"Looking at what happened today, I am not sure he fits the bill."

"But why?" he had a puzzled look on his face.

"Well, I only donated a five hundred grand compared to the two million you donated yourself."

"Oh for heaven's sake…you had me there for a second," he smiled and came closer to tell something…the power of the musky fragrance he wore, overtook her senses, "you know some of these women are wearing jewels worth the GDP of any small African nation, but if I reveal to you what they donate in the name of charity, my dear your father in comparison to these people…is a king for sure."

Aadvi was taken aback by what Sean had just said. She looked around, were these people really that miserly?

"So tell me Aadvi, what brings you to the greatest city in the world?"

"I am here on business, trying to settle here for as long as I can," a hint of sadness in her voice, "and it's stupid to ask you, what you are doing here?"

"Well even I am unsure of what I am doing here amongst these gold diggers? I would rather be at home, watching sports center. Would've left earlier after dropping the cheque had they not made me the guest of honor tonight."

Watch sports center or be on a date with a bimbo?

"Given your devotion to charitable activities how do you find time for recreation?" She tried to be cheeky.

"I try my best…I like to read, paint, travel…but as per the press and media, the only recreation I induge in, involves the company for models and escorts…and as per them, I have lots of time for that, thus it hardly qualifies as recreation." Aadvi was impressed by his upfront and direct attitude, neither shying away nor justifying his actions.

"We'll I am calling it a night…" as she placed her empty glass on the counter, "…else, Amigo will be furious."

Sean was confused and curious.

"Sounds like you have a special someone waiting for you?"

"Oh yes, he is pretty special alright…Amigo is my three month old French bulldog."

He had a relieved smile across his sexy face. They stared at each other, smiling. There was so much to talk about, so much to know about each other, but both were unsure of where to start.

"It was a pleasure meeting you Sean." she extended her hand.

"The pleasure was all mine." he shook her soft as silk hand.

It was a purely magical moment.

Oh God! She's beautiful!

At that very moment, someone called Sean's name and they were free of the spell of each other's eyes.

"Bye Sean, goodnight."

"Goodnight, see you soon."

Aadvi made her way towards the exit where the chauffeur waited with the car.

She sat in the car, looking back at the hall, where she had just met a charismatic young man, a heady cocktail of poise and good looks.

She was still tad wary of him and decided not to let her heart take control of her mind like last time.

Once bitten, twice shy…

But wanted to know more about the man who drove the females crazy that night. Despite what the tabloids said, the there was something irresistble about him.

Aadvi reached the Penthouse, where Amigo was restlessly waiting for her. She changed her clothes, slipping into a set of light pink silk pajamas.

She was starving and went to the kitchen to make a sandwich. Lost in a conversation with Sean, she forgot all about dinner.

She finished her sandwich; picked up Amigo and headed for the bed. It had been an exhausting day that had ended with an exciting night.

Her eyelids were extremely heavy; she stretched out her hand to switch off the light in the nightstand…looking forward to a tranquil Sunday.

CHAPTER 7

It was a slightly cloudy morning, a little breezy, with sparks of sunshine in between basically a perfect day to spend in the park. Amigo was happily playing with his chew toys or rolling on the floor, he could make out from the preparations that he was going out.

Aadvi picked up the picnic basket a few toys for Amigo, a book to immerse herself in.

11:00 am…they reached Central Park. The place was bustling with life. Couples young and old holding hands, kids having a ball, families just letting go of their problems in the past week and enjoying themselves with picnic baskets.

She found a perfect spot, placed a blanket and settled down. She let Amigo loose. He ran around joyfully with his chew toy in the mouth. Aadvi, who was casually, dressed in a royal blue tee and stonewashed denims, hair tied neatly in a ponytail, black wayfarers sitting perfectly on her beautiful face, immersed herself in a book whilst enjoying a sandwich.

"Hello Ms.Kapoor!"

She heard a familiar voice and looked back to find Sean Whitman standing in front of her with his Golden Retriever and a Frisbee grasped in the hand.

Dressed in a White tee and blue jeans and aviators…simple, sober and yet so sexy.

"Oh Hello, Sean, how are you doing and who is the cutie pie with you?"

"I am fine…and this guy here is my buddy Romeo."

"Romeo…hmm…has he found his Juliet yet?"

"Nah…neither him…nor me!" he said with a wily smile.

What is he hinting at?

People noticed him…he had such a recognizable face!

He lets Romeo loose and threw him the Frisbee which he gladly retrieved.
"It's a great day, isn't it?" he looked at her.

"It sure is."

"You live nearby?"

"Yeah on the East End Avenue, Upper East Side."

"Oh…So we are practically neighbors! I live on the Upper East Side as well…York Avenue"

Sean threw the Frisbee again. Aadvi offered him a soda, which he gladly accepted.

"You come here often?" she asked him.

"At least I try to!"

"So you live alone?" he gets inquisitive.

"Yes, my father sent me here for a project to work on. What about you, you work independently or with your father?"

"I am actually more of a creative guy, I want to start a clothing line soon, which I plan to design myself."

"Wow, a painter, a traveler, a designer …so do you plan to model for it too…coz with your looks, you surely can!"

Oh God…What did I just do? Did I really say that? Oh God… What was I thinking?

She was surprised at herself.

"Oh no…though it may not seem, from my character certificate made by the media…I am a simple guy. Thanks for the compliment though."

There was a shy smile across her face as she gazed at him.

After a while they left the park and headed towards their cars when Sean asked her something out of the blue.

"Aadvi, would you like to have dinner with me tonight?"

She didn't know what to say. She hardly knew him. It was an awkward moment, out of the blue this charming guy, who she'd just, met a few hours ago, asked her out and she didn't understand what to say.

Sean could sense Aadvi's hesitation.

"Hey…if you're not comfortable, it's ok…I get it we hardly know each other and I just asked you all of a sudden." His captivating eyes looked apologetic.

She stopped and thought for moment and blurted out, "yes…I would like that."

Sean looked happy, "Great, I'll pick you up at 7…it's a date!"

They exchanged phone numbers and Aadvi, texted him the address.

While driving back, she was surprised at herself, "What happened back there?" she murmured to herself, Amigo looked at her with amusement.

Amigo looked tired and hungry by the time they reached home. She fed him a hearty bowl of his favorite food. It was almost 4. She lay down on the couch, pulled up a throw blanket, set an alarm and closed her eyes for a quick nap.

The alarm woke her up and it was already 5.30. Aadvi rushed to her the closet and found herself totally confused, but after much thought set her heart on a tan colored jumpsuit accessorized with a matching clutch and pearl earrings.

She looked elegant.

It was almost 6.30. She fixed Amigo's meal and anxiously waited for her "date" to arrive. She sat down for a while; thinking about how the day had turned out and where was this going?

Her phone rang. It was her mother.

"Hey Mom…how are you and how's Dad?"

"I am fine darling, so is your father…how are you and why do you seem so stressed?" being a mother she knew from the tone of her voice that something was bugging her.

"Nothing Mom, I have a date, he's due to arrive in 20 minutes or so."

"Are you seeing someone?"

"No… we met last night at the charity dinner which I attended on Dad's behalf."

"What's his name?" she asked gladly.

"Sean Whitman…is there a problem Mom?" Aadvi was skeptical about her mother's reaction.

"No…why would that be a problem dear?"

"Because he's an American!"

Aadvi was aware of her mother's old school thinking.

"It doesn't matter so long as you are happy." Preeti was happy that her daughter was trying to move on.

Ding-dong...

"Mom I think he's here...I got to go, will call you later...bye."

"Bye dear."

They both hang up and Aadvi went to open the door.

It was him...he looked very appealing, almost tantalizing in a denim duke shirt and ivy colored jacket and denims. What a treat for eyes.

He looked at her, "hey...you look great."

"So do you!"

He handed her a bunch of fresh cut, long stem red roses.

She accepted them and invited him inside.

It was just yesterday we didn't know each other and today, he's here at my place, bringing roses for me!

"Thank you, please come inside while I place these beautiful flowers in a vase."

"Sure."

He entered the place as Amigo rushed to greet him.

"Wow, he remembers me?"

"Yes he does."

Aadvi placed the flowers in a crystal vase and picked her clutch from the table.

"Shall we leave?" Sean looks at his watch.

"Yeah."

They left the Penthouse and went towards the elevator. They looked at each other…and were awkwardly silent for a few seconds. They reached the entrance of the building where the very courteous Sean, opened the door for her. He took the seat next to her as they drove off.

"So where are we going?'

"I have a table reserved at Nobu…Have you ever been there?"

"Not yet, heard a lot about the place but never got a chance to try it out, it's been crazy since I came here."

"Well there's always a first time…mind if I turn up the music system?"

"Sure go ahead."

Even the God's seem to setting the mood for them as Michael Buble's version of Sway played.

Aadvi unconsciously began humming it.

When marimba rhythms start to play, dance with me, make me sway, Like a lazy ocean hugs the shore, hold me close, sway me more.

"Do you like this song?"

"Yes I do, but more than the song I like Michael, what a silky voice?"

Who else do you like to listen to?"

"Bryan Hayland, Ben E.King, Frankie Valli, Ray Charles, Tony Bennett...it's a very long list and an old one too!"

"Yeah quiet a list of legends you've got there!"

"Old is gold, isn't it?"

"Agreed."

They reached Nobu, just in time. It was tad crowded, being a Sunday but since the reservation was in place, they had no trouble finding a great little spot by the window.

People recognized him instantly. Amid the whispers, the server handed them the menus, updating them on the specials. They skipped the specials and began browsing the menus.

"Any salad for the lady?" he asked looking at Aadvi.

"I'll have a Shashimi salad with Matsuhisa dressing"

"And for the gentleman?"

"I'll have a Lobster salad with lemon dressing…make sure it's not too spicy."

"Something to drink Sir?"

He ordered a bottle of trig point Merlot.

"Sure Sir."

"So Aadvi, tell me, what have you done so far in the greatest city on earth?"

"Honestly…nothing…I've been here twice with my parents, but only for a holiday as a kid…this time round it was different. When I came here some months ago, I was only looking to work, immerse myself in the colors and culture of this city, and I've not had much to do all due to work constraints."

"But you seem to be so young, you should be full of life… enjoying this phase not immerse yourself in work as you say…" he looked at her as though seeking answers, "it seems you were trying to escape from something."

Aadvi, looked at him with demure; evocative moments running through her mind.

Was she still carrying the burden of events in New Delhi? Was it so evident from her face?

Nevertheless, she was intrigued about the courtly man sitting across her; she wanted to know him...the real Sean Whitman. Was he really a playboy, as suggested by the tabloids or a genuine man misunderstood by the masses and misrepresented by the media?

She braved it all and carried on with the conversation.

"You are right...I was looking for an escape route. From whom I can't tell you right now, because I don't know myself!"

"Hey it's ok if you don't want to share...my mistake I shouldn't have brought up such a topic!"

"It's alright."

The salad arrived along with the wine.

As the evening progressed, both of them were enchanted in each other's company.

Aadvi was relaxed; her mind free from everything else right now and the overwhelming feeling of pure tranquility took over her.

Sean on the other hand, seemed lost in her captivating beauty. He was attracted to her magnetic charm.

If only my eyes could speak what my heart is feeling?

A thought shared by both of them.

They finished dinner, it was already 10.30 pm. Sean called for the cheque.

"Shall we leave?" he asked her with a heavy heart.

"Yeah." she said, although her mind was unwilling to.

The valet brought the car as and they both got seated and drove away.

"I hope your first time experience at Nobu was good, hope you liked the food?"

"Oh it was fabulous, it's a shame I've not been here before."

"So Aadvi, since you've not been around much on your current stay in New York, how about I show you around… quiet sure that I am a better guide than most."

"Really…I would appreciate that, thank you."

"Don't thank me yet…Have you been to Times Square yet?"

"Yeah, just once…with my cousins when they were here sometime back!"

"So let's start with Times Square…any day of your choice?"

"But won't that hamper your work?"
"No…not at all, it'll be silly of me if I am not able to make time for a someone as gorgeous as you."

She blushed.

"Hmm…Wednesday?"

"Done…I'll pick you up at 5.30, but where do I pick you from your office or your house?"

"How about home?" I am practically free the whole day, so I plan to come back early."

"Alright, it's a date."

"It's a date." and she gazed out of the window smiling.

CHAPTER 8

They were a few moments away from reaching her place and neither of them wanted the night to end. There was so much to know about each other that both of them tried their best to avoid the inevitable.

"Hey I didn't like the dessert there somehow, want to have an ice-cream or something?" he asked her, hoping to hear a yes.

"Sorry I don't feel like having one, it's a tad chilly tonight."

They were almost close to her building.

"Then how about coffee?"

"Why don't you come back to my place for that, I make pretty good cappuccino?"

"Sure!" he affirmed; his heart beating crazily, not wanting to part from her.

They reached the Penthouse; while Amigo snored away in his bed.

"Please make yourself comfortable!"

Aadvi went to the kitchen to make coffee, while Sean looked around the apartment. Shifting his focus on the wall full of her family photos.

After a few minutes, Aadvi walked in with coffee. She placed the tray on the table and filled a cup for him.

"What are you looking at?"

"Pictures of your family. I since I know your Dad, I could recognize him and can make out from the photos that the lady in the beautiful dress is your Mom." pointing a finger towards Preeti.

"Ain't she beautiful?"

"Oh yes definitely. Now I know where you get your looks from." He smiled at her.

"Oh! Stop it...and that's not a dress, that's a saree, a traditional outfit worn by married Indian women!"

"I bet you'd look good in that!

Aadvi handed him a cup and poured one for herself.

He took a seat on the couch; eyes darted towards her. Though she tried hard to avoid any eye contact, she just couldn't help it.

"Really, I mean it. I've traveled the world, met many beautiful women, but haven't seen beauty as striking as yours…I want to know you more everyday, every minute, every second."

Oh wow, how do I respond to that?

Aadvi didn't know what to say. Her inexperience in the matters of the heart was proving to be the hurdle and his playboy image didn't make things any easier.

They both chose to remain silent for remainder of the time.

Sean finished his coffee.

"Goodnight Aadvi…it was a great evening." He got up to leave. As he walked towards the door, Aadvi followed him.

"Hey Sean!"

A startled Sean looked back.

Aadvi came close to him and gave a peck on his warm cheek.

"Thank you for a lovely evening…goodnight."

Sean was jubilant while Aadvi looked elated at what just happened.

Maybe this was the new beginning she was hoping for…and maybe it was.

While Sean drove away gleefully while Aadvi went to the balcony, with a warm coffee cup in her hands and warm feelings inside her.

After months of agony, she was at peace and pledged not to look back, from there on.

8.30 am…the next morning; Aadvi was still in the bed when her phone rang.

It was Sean.

"Hey, good morning!'

"Good morning to you too. Hope I didn't disturb your sleep…did you slept well last night?"

"Yes, I did I was just about to get up and prepare breakfast."

"Why don't you hire help to do your housework?"

"I like doing the chores myself…keeps my mind off certain things. Anyway you are up early?"

"I couldn't sleep the whole night! Due to certain things!"

"Oh really?

"Oh Yes…"

Sean and Aadvi were on a mesmeric high.

"I had to work on a few designs...I will send the designs to a friend Henri in Paris who will review my work and suggest me ideas on how to improve upon them...the sooner I'll send those, the sooner I'll start with my dream project."

"That's good." she got up from the bed picked up Amigo and settled on the recliner in her room overlooking the window.

Oh what a beautiful, crisp morning it was.

"Hey, do you want to watch a movie this evening?"

"I really can't say right now, I have a meeting with a few executives today which will go well until 5 or 5:30!"

"C'mon...let's get the later show...say at 9."

Might as well give in!

"Well alright then."
"Superb...I'll pick ya at 8...we'll grab a quick bite and head for the movie."

"Ok, see ya at 8...don't be late."

"Oh, I won't be late, despite too much work on my plate and if I do get late, I know I'll surely meet my fate."

"Bravo bravo." she exclaimed while clapping.

"Thank you. Glad I could impress you."

"Hey, Amigo seems hungry, I gotta give him something to eat and prepare breakfast for *moi*...gotta hang up now...I'll see you tonight."

"Yeah...can't wait."

Aadvi hangs up albeit against her wish. She goes to the kitchen fills up Amigo's bowl with his kibbies and hits the shower. Through with her breakfast she gets her paperwork in order and leaves for the office.

While on her way to work Aadvi got a call from Preeti.

"Hello dear."

"Hi Mom."

"You sound happy?" today the maternal senses were telling her a different story about her daughter.

"Yes Mom...I know why have you called at this hour...don't worry...the dinner went well."

"And how did you find Sean?"

"He's a great guy, so sensitive and caring, and very thoughtful, as I saw on the night of the charity dinner."

"Will you see him again?"

"Well..."

"I can make out from your tone that you'll see him soon!"

"Well, we are meeting tonight for a movie…let's see how it goes."

"Just don't over think, go with the flow…I know you very well darling…do what your heart tells you. God bless you."

"Yes Mom, don't worry…I've reached the office…must go, take care, bye and love ya." and she hangs up.

Despite her best efforts, she just couldn't work. Her thoughts focused on the "date" tonight and eyes fixated on the clock.

On the other hand Sean was even more restless and was unable to concentrate on work. It was unlike him.

His mind was completely overtaken by her thoughts.

I've dated so many women before, I've never felt this way about anyone, why is that with her I feel… different?

He was lost in her thoughts, when suddenly his phone rang.

It was from call from India.

It was Aadvi's father.

"Hello, Sean Whitman"

"Hello Sean, it's Rajan Kapoor."

"Hello Mr.Kapoor, how are you Sir."

"I am fine Sean…so you met Aadvi."

"Yes she's a great girl Mr.Kapoor." Sean was a little uneasy considering he was the father of the girl who made her heart beat like a drum, every time he saw her.

"Sean, I wanted to extend my donation to the Home Sweet Home project!"

"Why Sir, did Aadvi ask you to?"

"Oh no, I haven't spoken to her at all. In fact I was planning to call her right now. She'll give you another cheque tonight."

"Alright Mr.Kapoor…uh…what…tonight?"
He was stunned that Rajan knew about their date and was surprisingly calm.

"Oh come on I know you guys are going out tonight for a movie. Well I didn't speak to Aadvi, but that doesn't mean her Mom didn't!"

He took a deep breath and mustered courage, "Mr.Kapoor, are you fine with…this?"

"Sean you have my blessing, so long as my daughter is happy and I know she is…take care of her, bye." Rajan hangs up.

He knows and yet he is calm about it, God knows what she told her mother about me?

Still the conversation boosted his morale. At least his ethnicity was no problem with her family, something that withheld him to convey his feelings to her openly. He was at ease now hoping to turn over a new leaf.

CHAPTER 9

Aadvi reached home at 6 and slipped into a comfortable pair of denim top and jeans. Made a cup of tea and headed to the balcony with Amigo next to her. The early autumn breeze set the mood…perhaps a sign of things to come. After a long time she had an expression of positivity on her face.

With Sean I feel so much at ease. He makes me smile, I feel so happy when I am around him…there is no pressure with him.

Her phone rang, as she expected it was Sean.

"Hey"

"Hey you…I'll be there in five, are you ready?"

"Yup, so I'll see ya downstairs?"

"Why…you don't want me to come upstairs?"

"Oh! I didn't mean that…"

"Hey, hey…I was just kidding…now hang up and meet me downstairs."

"See ya."

Aadvi hung up the phone, filled up Amigo's bowl with food and bid him goodbye while he sulked at the sight of her leaving.

Sean waited for Aadvi outside the car. As she arrived, he moved forward and hugged her. She was pleasantly surprised and pulled him towards herself reciprocating his feelings. They broke the hug as he proceeded to open the door for her.

"You must be hungry?"

"Yeah…famished."

"What would you like to eat?"

"Hot dog and soda would be fine!"

"What?" he was surprised at her answer.

"There are better places and stuff to eat you know."

"Yeah but the point is to fill stomach with food. The stomach doesn't know where we are sitting and what are we eating."

"Hmm…that's quiet a theory you have…alright then, let me take you for the best hot dogs in New York…Gray's Papaya!"

"The name sounds interesting"

They drove towards the Upper West Side. The popular hot dog joint was already crowded. He ordered hot dogs and freshly squeezed orange juice to drink. They took a seat, on a nearby bench.

"That's a great hot dog," she said, wiping of the chili off her mouth, sipping on her orange juice.

"Yeah, it's a great place, thanks to you I am coming here after ages…reminds me of the times simpler times I spent here with friends, shared some great moments. Heck, I had forgotten how simple life is. How something as small as a hot dog can bring you a moment of happiness." He sighed.

"So how is Romeo?"

"He's fine…left him with a neighbor, she likes taking care of him."

"She…Hmm?" Aadvi was inquisitive.

"What are you hinting at Missy…My neighbor is a 60 year old grand mother of two!"

"I am kidding Mr. Whitman!"

They both shared a hearty laugh.

This feels so right!

They both liked each other's company, their eyes spoke a thousand words but the lips were sealed.

"You know Aadvi, I want to be honest with you about something's that have happened in the past."

He had vowed not to treat what he had with Aadvi like any other frivolous relationship from his past and try his best to make it work.

"Sean," she placed her hand on his cheek, "I don't want to know, what's in the past is in the past…you can't go back in time and change it so what's the point discussing it."

"No I have to say it…I really like you and I feel…you like me too?"

"Yes…yes I do."

"So I want us to start on a fresh note…come clean about each other's past" he moved on with his confession,

"I've dated a lot of women in the past but with them it was always, fast cars and fancy restaurants. I came out of a very messy realtionship a few months ago but we broke up due to her over demanding and overbearing attitude. Guess she was with me only for the money. Today I realize that I've wasted a lot of time on meaningless relationships…But your simplicity, your persona, everything about you is what makes those women shallow in comparison…you are the kind of woman, the woman of substance that I've hoped of finding all my life…"

"I feel so alive with you, no facade, no superficiality, I can be myself..."

She listened to him with intent. He took her hand and gazed in her eyes.

"I've always seen a certain amount of sadness in your eyes as if you are seeking closure from something...I want to know more about you...open your heart to me Aadvi."

Aadvi closed her watery eyes.

It's now or never Aadvi, just speak, clear your mind and let it out...

"Sean," she paused, "it's the same with me...I've seen a lot of mess around me in the last few months...It's better I come clean with you too and not only because I like you, but also because I want to make it work this time." she cleared her throat,

"I really liked a guy back in India...he was the son of my Dad's very dear friend...I met him at a party earlier this year and it was love at first sight, at least for me. He told me he was in love with someone else...but since the girl was an American citizen, a model I knew his parents would never allow him to marry her. My father and grandfather pitched the idea of getting us married but he out rightly refused, to point of offending his parents, knowing it will humiliate his father."

"He said he only saw me as a friend and nothing more than that...I had to give in eventually and solely for the sake of friendship, I backed out and the whole 'charade' as he called it, came to an end."

She began sobbing, hands covering her face, which had turned red.

Sean cuddled her in his arms, trying to console her, his eyes filled with love and compassion for her.

"Hey hey, listen…I believe everything happens for a reason and who knows you being here with me in this moment is what the universe wants. It's his loss that he couldn't see the purity of your heart but you will gain something so great…we will make it great." he kissed her forehead, comforting her.

"Well, we both have baggage that we are carrying and slowly but steadily we'll lose it all…don't worry."

Aadvi stopped crying and just peered into his beautiful eyes, begging one question and one question only

Sean Whitman…where have you been all my life?

She wanted to kiss him so badly, but something held her back, what and why she failed to understand.

"Let's go, it's 8.15…you don't want to be late for the movie do you?"

"No"

They got up from the bench and walked towards the car. After a few minutes, they reached the AMC Theater. Sean fetched the tickets and they made their way to the show.

Sean was overjoyed to have found someone to share the simpler joys of life with, he held Aadvi's hand and Aadvi, she was just…happy. Whatever the tabloids said, didn't matter, whatever anyone thought didn't matter.

After the show ended and the newest couple in town now headed home. Aadvi didn't want the night to end…but she had to let him go. He held her hand in the car and kissed it while listening to "Stand by me" playing on the CD.

"What are you thinking?" he inquired kissing her hand one more time.

"Is it really happening…we didn't even know each other a week ago!"

"Magical…isn't it?"

"It sure is." she clenched his hand.

"Hey I got a call from your Dad today."

"Really…but what for?" she sounded surprised.

"Apparently he wants to make another sizeable donation to our project."

"I hope you don't think I asked him to?"

"I didn't say you did…relax."

"But did he…" before she could say further.

"Yeah he did, he knows…but was calm about it."

"And what about you?" she asked with a tense look.

"Oh…I was sweating bullets…badly nervous!"

She laughed at his reaction.

"I am glad he knows." She was much more at ease now.

They reached home and she invited him inside.

"Coffee?"

"No…I think I'll pass today…don't want the coffee to keep me awake…right now I just want to go home and sleep as I think of you for some really sweet dreams."

He came closer towards her, stroked her hair. His eyes were fixed on her's, which lit up thinking about the next minute.

And before she could even think any further, he sealed her pink lips with a mesmerizing kiss…the first kiss…the long passionate kiss…that awesome moment that made her heart throb.

For Sean the moment was enthralling…he'd kissed slew of beautiful women in the past but none compared to the infallible beauty of this girl before him. What he shared with Aadvi at that point in time was the defining moment of his life as though, it was all he'd been waiting for.

Lips sealed with a lip-lock, arms settled on his shoulders and eyelids closed, she melted in his arms like a candle. His hands on her waist pulled her closer every second.

All of a sudden Amigo walked in on them, barking away at Sean as though feeling jealous. Sean and Aadvi couldn't help but laugh as she picked him up.

"I think he's hungry."

"No I think he's jealous!" he patted Amigo, "I got to head home."

He kissed her goodnight and left with love in his heart, smile on his face and spring in his step.

Aadvi went to her room to change, slipping into her pale blue silk pajamas, she retired to bed with her face beaming and eyes dreaming.

She deserved to enjoy every second of it...after all...she was in love.

CHAPTER 10

As any dutiful boyfriend would do, Sean called Aadvi, first thing in the morning.

"Good morning sunshine."

"Good morning…except that, there is no sun out today, so no sunshine."

"For me there is…so what are your plans for today?"

"I have to finish a lot of pending work today or Kutty my manager will be after my life."

"Work comes first…finish your work so that you can make time for us…want to meet up after 8?"

"Sure…why don't you come over to my place…I'll cook!"

"Would love to…would you like me to bring something?"

"Just ask my boyfriend to be on time."

"Don't worry, he'll be on time…fully at your service."

"Uh huh…" she was momentarily distracted as Amigo's antics took over their conversation, "I gotta hang up now, my other boyfriend is tugging away at my blanket for his kibbies."

"Please go ahead and take care of my nemesis. See ya babes."

"Bye"

They hang up, lost in each other's thoughts.

It was such a marvelous morning… everything seemed so new, so fresh, and so clear…so lovely.

Despite the slowpoke love makes one, Aadvi managed to get ready and reached office in time to tackle Kutty who was eagerly waiting for her.

"Good morning Aadvi?" Karen, one of the executives greeted her, on front door.

"Good Morning Karen."
"Good morning everyone!" she announced her arrival with an unusual exuberance.

She entered her cabin only to find a pile of papers waiting for her and Kutty knocking on her door.

"Come in"

"Good morning Kutty!"

"Good morning Aadvi…what happened you seem very happy?"

"Nothing much Kutty. I think it's the weather." she smiled at him.

Kutty couldn't understand what had happened to the usual Aadvi who walked in with a stern look on her face practically everyday.

"Aadvi…here are the papers we need to go over today, which we couldn't do yesterday in the meeting. We have to conclude this today as the final report has to be urgently sent to Rajan Sir."

"Don't worry Kutty, I will finish all the work today… happy?"

"More than happy I am relieved…I'll take leave now, I have to finish some work."

He exited the room closing the door behind.

Aadvi's phone rang; it was Avantika on the line.

"Hello my dear friend… how are you doing?"

"Hello Aadvi…wow someone is in a good mood and I think that special someone has found someone special."

"Oh! You are so right. But how do you know?"

"Preeti Aunty spoke to me the other day. So who's the guy?"

"His name is Sean Whitman but I won't tell you anything more than that."

"But why?" Avantika was puzzled, as Aadvi was not the one to hide anything from her.

"First tell me when are you coming to New York as you promised me?"

"Aadvi, that's why I called, to tell you that I am coming tomorrow…I'll land at 5:15 at JFK."

"Great, I'll pick you up, what's the flight number?"

"The flight number is QF 11"

"I hope Rajesh is coming with you!"

"Yes he is coming and now tell me about Sean."

Just then there was a knock on the door, it was Karen who wanted some input from Aadvi over an issue.

"Avantika, I gotta hang up, some important work has come up and as far as telling you about him goes…we can continue our talk when you come here. I'll see you tomorrow."

"See you tomorrow."

The day passed quickly. Aadvi left the office and made a stop at a nearby store to pick up a few things for dinner. She was excited to cook for Sean and for the first time her mind was not playing games with her. She was free of doubts, even though she knew they were moving at a very fast pace.

She reached home to find a sleepy Amigo who was too lazy to even open his eyes. Only two hours to go till Sean arrived and she hadn't even started yet. She changed quickly into casual clothes, tied an apron and began cutting veggies for the salad and boiled the chicken. She was running out of time, but managed to finish the food just in time to take a quick shower and change into some respectable and odorless clothing.

Aadvi inspected the place since Amigo was in the habit of leaving his chew toys around. The Penthouse was sparkling clean. She arranged the lighting to suit the mood.

It was time and Sean was right on dot. The bell rang and Aadvi rushed to open the door to find the most handsome man in New York with a bottle of Cabernet Sauvignon in one hand and a bunch of beautiful red roses in the other.

"Hey beautiful"

"Hello handsome" she welcomed him with a kiss.

He followed her inside like an infatuated puppy.

"You are right on time, your punctuality is a great feature about you."

"Couldn't afford to be late for our first dinner together as a couple" he said taking a seat on the couch and pulled her by her hand towards him. She settled next to him placing her head on his shoulder.

"But first, let's untie this bun." He referred to her hair, "I like your hair open."

"What would you like to drink?"

"What do you have?"

She pointed towards the bar "help yourself and pour me some wine while I fix the appetizers, hope you like your food spicy."

He grinned and winked at her, "Oh yes, I like spicy stuff."

Aadvi kissed him and made her way to the kitchen.

Sean walked to the bar and fixed his scotch, on the rocks and poured Aadvi a glass of the Sauvignon as she walked in with a platter of cottage cheese tikka's, chicken kebabs and oven roasted mushrooms.

"Looks yummy."

"Hope you like it!"

Sean picked up a fork and helped himself.

"Wow the chicken is fantastic, now let me try another one."

Aadvi picked her glass, happy to see Sean enjoying the food, "be my guest"

"Don't worry about me."

She remembered something, got up and went to her room, only to bring a cheque of additional $ 5,00,000 as promised by Rajan.

"Oh God, I told your Dad not to do it but seems he a stubborn man!"

"Hey don't say anything against my father…" she punched him jokingly.

"Sean, there's some news." she had his attention; "I think we won't be able to go to Times Square tomorrow!"

Sean was concerned "but why?"

"Nothing to be so concerned…it's just that my best friend called in from Sydney today, she's coming to New York tomorrow with her husband for a few days and I gotta pick her up in the from JFK at 5.15 in the evening."

"It's fine…take care of your friend, if you say I'll come along with you."

"Really?"

"Yeah sure…anything for you babes."

"Avantika will be thrilled to meet you. She got married this year but I couldn't be at her wedding since I lost my grandfather just two days before that…" she seemed lost thinking about the time gone by and the hurtful turn of events after that.

Sean snapped her out of it.

"Hey…where did you just fly off to without me?" while his hand stroked her face.

"Nowhere, I am right here next to you." she took Sean's hand in her's.

"You want me to put on some music?" She asked him softly.

"Sure…Michael?" He knew she liked his voice.

"Buble or Jackson?" she teased him.

"I am a pretty good dancer you know, but sure as hell can't do a Moonwalk!"

Aadvi giggled.

"So Buble it is!"

Her sweet voice and pleasing smile just melted his heart.

"Exactly!"

She walked up to the music system and shuffled through some albums
And found the perfect song to set the evening going...
Moondance.

"Do you want to dance?" he got up form the couch walking towards her.

"Sure." she extended her hand.

"Well, it's a marvelous night for a moondance
with the stars up above in your eyes
a fantabulous night to make Romance
'neath the cover of October skies..."

Her big brown eyes met his grey ones.

"I wish this night never ends..." he sighed looking at her.

"Me too... but unfortunately it has to."

They continued dancing with their lips close to each other; a moment ruined by a phone call Sean received.

What does he want now?

"Hello...yeah hi Dad...yes...don't worry I'll be there."

It was a brief phone call, which surprised Aadvi, since a guy as loving and caring as Sean literally neglected his father.

He looked disturbed...

"Hey, what happened, you look concerned?"

Since he didn't want to bother Aadvi, he changed the subject.

"Hey, what happened, you look concerned?"

"Oh it's nothing dear…just some official stuff." he gulped down his scotch and headed to the kitchen, "come on, I am starving…what are we having for dinner?"

"Well…butter chicken which is a North Indian specialty, cottage cheese in tomato and onion gravy and steamed rice and Indian bread, which you will have to wait for!"

"Sure but what about dessert?" he tried to catch her playfully across the kitchen counter.

"I got some ice cream of you like!" the naughty side of things took control; she tried to get away from him.

"What if I want something else." he teased her… trying to reach out his hand to her.

She caved in when caught.

Sean hugged her, expressions changing again on his face, 'no need to make the bread, just rice would be fine…let's eat, I gotta leave soon."

"But why…that too all of a sudden?"

He flashed his phone at her, "Dad's call remember, gotta sort out some stuff, have to see my parents in the morning."

She heaved a heavy sigh and set the table.

Sean looked out the window lost in his thoughts. After a few minutes Aadvi, called him to join her at the table. Sean served her more wine and got another scotch for himself as he took a seat.

"Hope you like it!" She served the food.

"Hmm…I can easily tell the food is fantastic." he says lost in the aroma from the steamed saffron rice with a hint of cardamom.

"Don't just look at it…dig in."

"As you say M'lady"…he took a few bites relishing the food," Wow, you really know the way to a man's heart is through his stomach!"

"Yes I do!"

"What about the way to a woman's heart?" his look beckoned an answer.

"Ceaseless love!" she declared with a smile.

The evening passed quickly, as time to bid goodbye dawned closer. Aadvi and Sean parted with a tender kiss with Sean promising her to meet the next day.

After Sean's departure, Aadvi got a call from her mother.

"Hey Mom"

"Hello darling, so how's my Princess doing?"

"Fine Mom."

"Avantika's father called today and spoke to Rajan, she's coming to New York tomorrow."

"Yes Mom she already spoke to me this evening."

"Take good care of her, will you, don't get engrossed in work or Sean."

"Mom…"

"By the way how is he?"

"You just missed him, he was over for dinner, left about 5 minutes ago."

"You sound happy!"

"Absolutely Mom, he's a wonderful guy."

"Well baby, I am happy if you are happy…anyway, it's quiet late, you better sleep now."

"Yeah good night Mom, love you."

Aadvi headed to her room to change as Amigo followed her lazily from his bed and and lied down near her bed on the mat. She patted him while pondering about the sudden change in Sean after that phone call.

In a few moments her droopy eyes gave up and she dozed off.

CHAPTER 11

The next morning was chaotic. Worn out from last night's dinner, Aadvi was too lazy to get out of the bed while Amigo barked and tugged away her blanket. Aadvi in utter frustration got up and changed putting off the shower for later.

She had to make sure the room was well set for Avantika and her husband who were going to stay with her for the duration of their time in New York.

She went for the supermarket to stock up on food, veggies and fruits etc. Given her schedule, she hardly went to a supermarket. On her way, she called up Kutty to inform him about her plans for the day.

"Hello Kutty."

"Yes Aadvi, you are quiet late today, hope everything's alright?"

"Yes Kutty, everything's fine…it's just that I am not coming in today…will you manage on you own, I have some guests coming over from Australia and will be caught up with them for a few days."

"Yes Aadvi, I'll manage, please enjoy your time with guests."

"Let me know if you need my input on something… don't shy away from calling me.

"Sure…but there are a few papers you need to look at, shall I email those to you?"

"Or better yet, I'll come over to the office as I just remembered I need some important files, I'll pick those and have a look at those papers as well." She gets a call on the other line, "Kutty, I am getting another call, gotta hang up…bye."

It was Sean.

"Hello babes, good morning."

"Good morning Love…slept well?"

"It was like I was roofied…was it you Aadvi?"

"No it wasn't me…could be one of your other girlfriends"

He could hear her snicker.

"There are no other girlfriends Ms. Kapoor…you are my one and only!"

"Oh really, is that so?"

"Uh huh…Hey, what time should I meet you at the airport or should I pick you up from your place?"

"I'll meet you at the airport at 5 as I need to make a quick stop at the office to collect a few files."

"Why can't you just take a break, now that your friend is coming over?"

"Yes I really need a break but this is more important than a vacation right now."

"Alright missy, finish your work and I'll see you at the airport. Love you"

"Bye! Love you."

Running from pillar to post taking care of errands exhausted her, she carried on nevertheless, for seeing her best friend after months and making her stay as comfortable as possible was the only thing on her mind.

She reached home at 1.30, took a long hot bath, a 30-minute power nap and she was good to go. Meanwhile Amigo who had already been fed, could sense someone was coming over since he kept on sniffing and whimpering at the door of the room prepared for Avantika and Rajesh and Aadvi was trying her best to keep him away from it.

"Amigo, you better is on your best behaviour." She warned him.

It was already 4. She called for the car and asked her chauffeur to head towards the office. The busy bee that she was, she still managed to finish work she reached JFK just in time.

Sean spotted her. She reached out to him and they hugged each other. Before she could say anything a voice called out Aadvi's name.

It was Avantika along with her husband Rajesh.

"Avantika, wow you look fabulous." both friends embraced each other, "and Rajesh Mehta, the guy who stole my best friend." she hugged him as Sean looked on.

Avantika noticed a fine-looking stud standing next to Aadvi.

"This must be Sean!"

Sean greeted Avantika and Rajesh and they made a move for the car, but Sean excused himself and promised Aadvi to join them later for drinks back at the Penthouse.

Though Aadvi sat in the car, her mind was someplace else. She was perplexed due to Sean's mysterious attitude since last night. She had been meaning to ask him what was eating him away, but the existing circumstances wanted her to look after her friends.

I will talk to him…but when the time is right!

They reached the Penthouse at 6.45 and are introduced to Amigo who seemed irked to find new faces at 'his' house.

"Hello little guy," Avantika was excited to meet him.

The couple made themselves comfortable on the couch, while Aadvi went to the kitchen to prepare tea for all of them.

She served the tea and took a seat next to the couch as the childhood friends began to catch up.

Rajesh, Avantika's husband was an investment banker with a firm in Sydney. He was an old schoolmate of Aadvi and Avantika's high school sweetheart. When his father moved to Australia, Rajesh was still in high school. He left India but could never leave Avantika's love behind. They set the perfect example of how long-distance relationships should be maintained. After Rajesh's parents died in car crash, he became lonesome and headed to Delhi to meet Avantika, where he proposed her.

"So Aadvi, tell us about Sean."

"Sean has been nothing short of a magician for me. Can you believe we've only known each other a week and it seems like a lifetime! The circumstances during which I came to New York were very difficult, metally and emotionally. Sean has helped me get over those…Love heals you in ways medicines can't."

Rajesh nodded to what she said, "I can totally relate to that, since I have gone through the same roller coaster of emotions when my parents died and Avantika helped me get over it…she told me about your situation and I am glad you found someone so caring…he seems like a nice guy."

"Thanks…hey you guys must be tired, let me show you your room and make sure you don't let Amigo in or he won't let you relax. It takes time for him to settle once he sees new faces." she informed them of the night's plan, "Sean will come over at 9, would you guys prefer eating hear or would like to go out?"

Rajesh who seemed too drained, "better if we stay back and order, it was a tiring 21 hour flight with a stopover at Los Angeles."

Aadvi showed them their room.

"Whatever suits you two, relax, catch-up on some sleep."

They settled their luggage in the room and Aadvi moved to her room to take a quick nap considering how drained she was after the day's activities.

8.30 pm…Aadvi though still bushed, woke up and headed to the kitchen to arrange some appetizers and ordered the food from a nearby restaurant.

The clock struck 9 and Rajesh who was now awake, headed to the bar and made a drink for himself since his workload didn't give him much time to unwind he looked forward to make most of this vacation. He was relaxed today, enjoying the crisp October breeze on the deck.

The doorbell rang; it was Sean at the door. Aadvi greeted him with a quick kiss.

"So you guys had some much needed rest?" Sean asked Rajesh as they shook hands.

"Yes...I am still low on energy though...so it will be early lights out for us tonight, since it was exasperating flight."

"What will you have Sean?" Rajesh who stood next to the bar took on the bartending duty for the night while the women took care of the food.

"Scotch, on the rocks and for my love sweating it out in the kitchen, some Merlot please." he pointed out to her as she blew him a flying kiss.

Avantika, who was now out of the kitchen, plugged the music system to put on some classic Kenny G to set the mood right.

Rajesh looked at her with an inviting smile and made her a Cuba Libre.

Love was in the air...two-love struck couples, relishing these moments of sheer bliss.

The drinks were ready and so were the cocktail snacks.

"So Sean, Aadvi was telling us about your influence on her. What do you have to say about her influence on you?"

Sean looks at her, lost in her beauty.

"Intoxicating. Her influence on me has been simply…
intoxicating. Can't think about anything else when I am
with her. As strange as it may seem or sound, since the day
we've meet, I just can't get her out of my head…I am under
her influence 24 /7."

To hear these words coming especially from Sean was a
pleasing moment for her. All the pieces of the puzzles were
falling into right places, but the 'mystery' surrounding him
still eluded her.

The evening ended as the dinner went superbly well. Aadvi
and Sean were happy to have found good company in Rajesh
and Avantika.

"Well it's time for me to push guys…it was great meeting you!"

Sean bid them goodnight as he made his way to the door.

"Thank you for finding time for all of us today. It meant a
lot to my friends!"

"Hey I wanted to be here more than you did…they are
a great couple, let's make plan this weekend and go to
Hamptons with them. All of us could use a break!"

"But isn't it too soon?"

"It is…but I really want us to find some time alone, away
from the your office, files, phone calls and I need to get rid
of the sketchbook and the pencil…its driving me nuts!"

"Alright...let me talk to them...will let you know tomorrow."

"Sure thing baby...goodnight, sweet dreams" and he leaned in to kiss her.

After he leaves, Avantika comes out of her room changed up, waiting for Aadvi to get free from the kitchen duty, so that the two friends could catch up.

"So tell me what's the deal with Sean, he seems enamored with you!"

"Yeah he is and I am crazy about him too."

"Yeah looks like it...a refreshing change for you from... you know whom," she continued, "have you been in touch with him?"

"No...that is one part of my life I wish never existed...but unfortunately it does...but I can't open an old book and read it again and again." she continued, "Life seems unfulfilled when you are alone. I am at point of my life where I feel the need of a companion more than ever. Having spent a good part of my life alone, I feel the need for someone more than my parents or a good friend...and Sean is just that...he's brought a sense of stability in my life"

'Your happiness is what matters Aadvi, devote yourself to this relationship, give it you hundred per cent."

"I will, I will."

"I know you Aadvi, you are too emotional…I am a little concerned for you."

"Well thank you dear…but don't worry, I got this."

Aadvi hugged Avantika, who had been like a sister to her all her life; looking out for her every time.

"Now you better get some sleep if you want to go for some sight seeing tomorrow."

"Ok…goodnight dear" Avantika moved to her room.

"Goodnight!"

Aadvi spent some time watching T.V. with Amigo resting his head idly on her lap.

She was glad to have some company in her otherwise empty place.

CHAPTER 12

Unlike recent days, the sun shone brightly over the city's skyline. Aadvi woke up to the dazzling sunshine in her room. It was 8.30. Amigo was fast asleep in his bed. Aadvi comes out to the living room rubbing her eyes and found Avantika and Rajesh romancing over tea.

"Good morning guys…having fun?"

They were startled.

"Good morning Aadvi" Avantika replied blushing.

Aadvi laughed," so this is what marriage does to you?"

"Why don't you find it for yourself…get married?" Rajesh teased her.

"It's too soon to walk that path!"

"It's never to late to find happiness!" Avantika joined the debate.

"Really can't say anything right now…we just started seeing each other, we are getting to know each other day by day. In an Indian set up it could've been possible, but with Sean who has been born and brought up here in West …for him it might be too early to talk about marriage."

"Still Aadvi, you never know!" Avantika chose to remain positive.

"Just cut it out guys…that reminds me Sean has planned something for the weekend…do you guys want to go to the Hamptons?"

"This weekend?" Avantika smiled.

"Yes, this weekend, why are you so amused?"

"Have you forgotten, it's your birthday on Saturday. Does he even know?"

"No, I haven't told him yet…heck, even I forgot all about it."

"Don't look too so shocked…these are the symptoms of L.O.V.E. my dear"

Aadvi rolled her eyes, "will you please cut to the chase and say yes to the plan. I want all of us to be together."
"Yes we will join you guys." Rajesh calmed her down.

"But a request guys, please don't tell Sean about my birthday, I don't want to feel pressurized into doing something special…as it is he's very busy with his work."

"Don't worry we won't tell him." Rajesh assured her, "but make sure he doesn't pay for of us."

"Rajesh, we can settle that later."

Aadvi was upbeat. It would be her first outing out of New York in months that too being her first with Sean. She called up Sean to convey the news of Avantika and Rajesh's willingness to come along.

"Hey sweetheart…good morning. "She was thrilled.

"Good morning babes, you seem excited."

"So I talked to Avantika and Rajesh and they are ready to join us for Hamptons!"

"That's great news…I'll make the reservations at the best hotel."

"Sean, wouldn't it be great if we spent our time at a cozy B & B rather than a hotel."

"Are you sure?"

Sean was amazed at her simplicity; flashes of his over demanding exes, who hassled him for trivial things, ran through his head.

"Yes! I am pretty sure!"

"Roger that…it's Thursday today, so we'll leave tomorrow evening from your place…can't wait to be with you!"

"Me too love…so what are your plans for today?"

"We I am working on my designs right now…have to take Romeo to the vet later, he's a bit under the weather!"

"Oh the poor guy…give him a kiss from me."

"Ok…what about me?"

"Hmm…don't kid yourself!"

He chuckled.

"So where are you guys headed to?"

"We are heading to 5th avenue as Avantika needs to do some shopping, followed by lunch and a Broadway show in the evening."

"That's quiet a workout for one day…hope you guys have fun."

"Will you be able to join us?"

"Can't babes, I need to finish all the work before we leave tomorrow, I want to spend my time with Aadvi my girlfriend, not the businesswoman, I request you to please, let loose for the weekend, no work, no stress, and no Kutty."

Aadvi couldn't help but let out a hearty laugh.

"Don't worry, I promise you, no work. Take care…I love you."

"Love you too."

Aadvi and her 'posse' changed, and after a quick breakfast left for the shopping spree. After reaching 5ᵗʰ Avenue and a couple of selfies later, the girls began their retail therapy with a helpless Rajesh carrying a look on his face as though, hit by a truck.

He could never understand his wife's the crazy love for branded shopping and though he inherited a lot after his parents passed away, he was still, a very practical guy who believed in saving for the rainy day and worked very hard for his money.

While the ladies, racked up huge bills at various high-end stores, Rajesh decided to explore the area alone. After a few hours, the famished duo of Avantika and Aadvi decided to call it off. Rajesh utilized his time well, roaming in surrounding area and suggested a place for lunch.

"While you ladies were out there 'enjoying your retail therapy' I decided to walk around the area and found out a great place to eat...let's go...I am starving!"

"So are we!" Aadvi responded with a groan.

They walked a few blocks to reach Ben & Jack's Steak House. As they got seated, Aadvi got a call from Sean.

"Hey, how's the shopping spree coming along?"

"Ah...Great, I am glad Avantika's trip was worth it, she found everything she needed, though Rajesh doesn't quiet agree with us."

"And why is that?"

"This first morning alone has been quiet heavy on his pocket."

Avantika teased him while Rajesh frowned.

"We're at Ben & Jack's Steak House in case you want to join us!"

"Sorry, gotta pass, I sent my designs to Henri and he's given me a great feedback. I could be well on my way to start the project in the next month or so. Lots of work to finish"

"That's great news. I am so thrilled for you."

"Thanks babe...I'm getting a call from Henri on the other line. I'll call you back."

"Yeah sure, bye love"

She conveyed the good news about Sean's designs to them.

"It's great...but isn't he son of a hotshot billionaire?" Avantika was curious.

"Yes he is...but Sean believes he can do without the family billions, he's a creative guy and wants to do something on his own...and I completely stand by him!"

Avantika looked at Aadvi with pride.

Aadvi looked at the watch, "hey don't you guys want to catch that musical, we should move our butts now."

They headed to the car and drove off to Broadway to catch 'Phantom of the Opera.'

After the spectacular show ended, the tired gang headed home, picking some take out on the way, as the ladies were too tired to enter the kitchen. Amigo welcomed Aadvi playfully barking at her as she picked him up, he licked her face and Avantika stood laughing at the scene.

"Well, you won't be needing makeup remover after that."

Rajesh placed food on the table; Avantika brought out the soda's form the refrigerator as they prepared to eat.

"Aadvi what time are we leaving for Hamptons?"

"We'll leave at 5, Sean will meet us here. Get your bags ready for tomorrow, I have to go to the office in the morning to take care of some stuff."

"Alright then, we can go to the Met." An all excited Rajesh literally jumped from his seat.

"Why Met?" Avantika was curious.

"When we left Sydney, we made it clear one day for you one day for me!"

"What does that even mean?" Aadvi was amused.

Avantika recalled and informed her, "before coming here we decided that one day we will engage in activities I like and the next day what his heart desires. Ok honey…the Met it is! Happy?"

"You bet I am!"

They finished dinner and headed for their rooms, too tired to even look at the shopping bags let alone take it with them.

In the morning, Rajesh and Avantika finished their breakfast getting up earlier than Aadvi and left a note on the refrigerator to inform Aadvi of their whereabouts. They planned to take a big bus tour of the city and then carrying on to Met.

Aadvi woke up to find them gone and helped herself to a toast and black coffee, showered and changed quickly so as to reach office in time to get rid of her pending work.

She was on top of the world, Sean hadn't called this morning but it didn't matter to her, she decided to look beyond these petty things, this what she'd promised to herself to make it work and if that meant overlooking some trivial things, then so be it.

She managed to reach office on time as Kutty welcomed her at her cabin door, with his usual exuberance. She informed him about her unavailability for the next few days.

"Kutty, since I won't be here for the next few days, take care of everything and no offence but don't call me for anything?"

The amiable South-Indian was taken aback.

"Don't look so shocked, I won't be able to take your calls."

"Point Taken." Kutty was relieved.

She asked him for help, "Can you please do me another favor?"

"Yes please tell me?"

"My French bulldog, Amigo needs a place to crash for the weekend, do you know anyone who will be happy to doggy-sit him?"

"No problem, he can stay at my place! My kids will be happy to see him!"

"What about your wife?"

"She's in Seattle for her cousin's wedding. I couldn't go with her due to the kid's school."

"Are you sure, you'll manage?"

"Oh yes of course! When should I pick him up?"

"It's almost 2 now, we'll leave at 3, be ready, because I am going out of town in the next couple of hours, so you come along with me to my place, get him and his stuff and Anderson my chauffeur will drop you back at your place, take rest of the day off…how does that sound."

"Yeah, that sounds great!"

Kutty left the room as she began dialing her mother informing her about the trip.

After failing to get through a couple of times she gave up and sent her a text.

Her phone pings and Aadvi finds some lovey-dovey messages from Sean. She reads each one again, and again, and again, blushing.

She finished her work just in time. It was 3. Aadvi called for Kutty and they left for the Penthouse. Avantika called her up to ask about her whereabouts.

"Aadvi where are you?"

"I am on my way, have you guys had lunch?"

"Yes we did, we came back an hour ago, to 'freshen up'!"

Aadvi heard Rajesh snickering in the background.

"Oh yeah, is that what they are calling canoodling these days? Freshen up?"

"Let's see how much do you freshen up the next few days?" Avantika taunted her jokingly.

"Oh shut up!" she hangs up, smiling to herself.

At the Penthouse, Kutty tried to be friendly with Amigo and he seemed to like him back. Kutty got his stuff and took it to the car while Aadvi got all emotional leaving him for the first time. She bid him goodbye with a heavy heart.

Sean arrived right on time with his Cadillac Escalade; good enough for the two couples to ride freely and comfortably.

The trip meant a lot for both couples. For Avantika and Rajesh, it meant some precious moments together after months, as Rajesh was always preoccupied with his work and Avantika being a homemaker was absorbed in taking care of the house until she got a job worthy of her competence.

For Aadvi and Sean, the trip was a medium of connecting with each other; to strengthen the bond, which was still in its infancy. Every thought, every second was tempting, away from everything, just the two of them.

CHAPTER 13

It was almost 7.45 by the time the couples reached 'The Mill House Inn' in East Hampton. Since the drive wasn't that long, they were fresh enough to check into their suites and meet at the restaurant for dinner. It was one of the Finest B & B's and Sean made sure they got the rooms with best views.

"Finally made it!" Aadvi was upbeat, "glad to have a break from the city life."

"And from work" Sean raised his glass to toast the freedom.

"To love and Romance which beckons all of us." Rajesh joined in.

The ambience of the place began working it's magic.

The food was scrumptious and the wine was smooth to get things going. The married twosome, made a move for their room, not wanting to waste any moment of the precious time they got together.

"Guys we'll see you at breakfast tomorrow…and enjoy yourselves…Goodnight." Avantika and Rajesh left the two of them alone.

Aadvi and Sean decided to take a stroll in the garden. Hand in hand, they moved further…looking at each other one moment, smiled and then looked straight ahead, the next.

"Seems too good to be true doesn't it?" Sean asked Aadvi.

"Yes it does! The place, this moment…God! It feels so surreal!" Aadvi just couldn't stop grinning, "It was a great idea to come here."

"We could've gone home too, you know?"

"You have a home…here in Hamptons?"

"Yes my father bought a property here a few years ago, it's more of a love shack for him!"

"So your parents come here often?"

"Honey, love shack doesn't necessarily mean he comes here with my mother!"

Aadvi was astounded.

"Don't look so surprised, my parents separated a few years ago."

She could see how hapless he felt…his eyes seeking answers… searching for something.

"Hey…now where did you fly off too?"

She tried to cheer him up. Sean passed her a saddened smile and hugged her tight.

"Come let's go to the room and order some wine…" Sean Lead her to their suite.

It was two-bedroom suite with a scenic view and delectably designed and had a glass fireplace.

But something bugged her.

"Sean…why the two bedroom suite?"

"Aadvi, I am not one of those guys who are just waiting upon an opportunity to jump in bed with women…and I wasn't sure if you'll be comfortable or not?"

"You thought that all Indian girls have a traditional approach to life…I won't be at ease…but I trust you." her comforting smile was enough to confirm her trust.

They ordered some fine Merlot as they sat on the couch next to the burning fireplace…her slim frame buried in his big arms and a blanket covering the hearts on fire.

She looked up to him…he seemed to drown in her big beautiful brown eyes, sheer perfection of her face made everything pale in comparison.

He moved forward to kiss her, hands tightly grabbing her waist and she reciprocated his act of passion by joining in.

"I love you!" he said breaking away from her luscious lips.

"I love you too!" she expressed her feelings as well.

Engaged in a heady lip-lock, they continued making out for sometime, before moving to their respective rooms even though against their wishes and neither of them brave enough to admit it.

In the morning, a perky Aadvi woke a little early, to witness the sunrise, to feel the clear, crisp air and see maple leaves spread across the garden like a carpet.

There was a knock on her bedroom door.

Why is Sean knocking on the door rather than walking in?

She walked across her bed to open the door, only to find the seating area of the suite filled with choicest of flowers… Roses, Lilies, Orchids, Carnations and a small box on the coffee table… gift-wrapped with a note next to it. Aadvi was getting increasingly inquisitive.

She looked around but finds no one there. She walked towards the table and opened the box with excitement to find a pair of majestic sapphire earrings from Tiffany's with the note saying, 'To my love, with all my love…Happy Birthday'.

Aadvi's was so riveted in the emotional moment, when a sudden hug from behind startled her.

"Happy birthday babes!"

She turned back to saw Sean looking at her and with those big sparkling eyes.

"Do you like the earrings?"

"I love them…but how'd you know that it's my birthday?"

"Well I made a call to your Dad, day before yesterday about some charity project and as luck would turn out, he spoke to me about your Birthday. And what better way to celebrate it, than here…in Hamptons."

"Well I love these but I love you more…", she was too overwhelmed.

She tugged his shirt to pull him closer and kissed him in a flash.

Their kiss, was short lived due to a knock on the door, it was Rajesh and Avantika. Sean opened the door and let them inside.

Avantika gave Aadvi a tight hug so did Rajesh. They gifted her two scarves; a pink and a traditional colored brown and gold with the original monogram, from Louis Vuitton, one of her favorite brands.

"Thank you so much guys."

"Wow! The room looks amazing Sean. Rajesh take note, my birthday is round the corner!"

"Whatever you say your highness." Rajesh bowed to her, with folded hands, "Sean don't give her any more ideas."

"Come on guys let's change and come to our room for the breakfast, the view from the deck is amazing. And the day is surprisingly sunny, so we'll go to the beach."

"That said…Avantika, you take a lot of time to shower and change…so you better move you butt." Rajesh knew his wife inside out.

"Ok guys we'll see you in our room." Rajesh and Avantika leave.

"Sean, why don't you get ready first, I have to sort out my clothes!"

"Why don't you join me?" trying to be his impish best.

"So you won't share a room with me but will make me an offer to join you in the shower…I don't think so mister." she pushed him towards the bathroom.

"Alright, alright, I am going."

He picked up his stuff and went to the bathroom.

Aadvi, in the meantime got out her clothes. A crimson colored top with beige Capri along with ruby studs set in 24-carat gold with a bracelet to match, both gifted by her mother. The earrings reminded Aadvi of her mother and she was lost in her thoughts when her phone rang.

It was Rajan.

She picks up the phone ecstatically, "Hey Dad!"

"Happy Birthday my Princess, God Bless You...wish you were here with us right now."

"Dad come on, it's not I am away from you for the first time and don't worry, I shall see you soon, I am coming home in December first week."

"That is great Princess… speak to you Mom."

"Hey Mom!"

"Wish you a very Happy Birthday my dear, God Bless You darling, I am missing you terribly." her voice cracking a bit.

"Mom, please don't cry, I told Dad I am coming home soon."

"No I am not crying, I am fine...how are you and how is Sean? Are Avantika and Rajesh with you?"

"Yes Mom, we are here at a Bed and Breakfast in Hamptons, Rajesh and Avantika are here with me and Sean...he made my birthday all the more special. I woke up to a room full of flowers and a pair of gorgeous sapphire earrings from Tiffany."

"That's great dear…but are you in the same room?" She sounded concerned.

"Mom we are in the same suite but separate rooms…Sean is great guy who knows his boundaries that too so early in the relationship. I trust him and you should trust me."

"Yes I trust you."

"Ok Mom I gotta go, we have to meet Avantika and Rajesh for breakfast."

"Alright darling, love you"

She hung up the phone and turned back to find a sight straight out of Greek mythology. Instead of a clothed up Sean, stood Adonis, the Greek good of beauty and desire, except that her Adonis wore a towel. Bulging biceps, beefy shoulders, chiseled body with washboard abs, messy hair dripping water droplets, oh what a fine specimen he was… she had always imagined in her mind how he would look shirtless, but could never fathom such a steamy sight.

I could faint any second now…get a hold of yourself, will you! But he looks so dishy…Oh…Stop it! Stop it! Stop it!

He stood in front of her grinning…almost teasing her.

"Wow, you're quiet a looker!"

"Oh really…told you to join me but…" the wicked grin back on his face.

"Alright now get dressed and let me go!" Aadvi rolled her eyes, smiling.

"Do I really need to? Can't I join you guys like this?" he took a chair, placing his muscular legs on the table, one top of the other.

"Hmm…it's my birthday and you'll go in your birthday suit?" she asked him raising her eyebrows.

"No problem, I'll get dressed and you join us in your birthday suit!"

"Hah…in your dreams buster…Boy, You're on fire today with the dirty jokes aren't you?"

"Aww…come on, it's ok to have some fun especially with your girlfriend!"

"Ok Mr. Whitman, waste your time horsing around, making silly jokes, while I will join our friends who must be waiting for us by now."

She turned around.

"Hey, I am sorry" he stopped her and held his ears to apologize, placed a fiery kiss on her lips, something she had been yearning from the moment she saw him out of the shower.

Moving away unwillingly, Sean made a move for his room.

Aadvi, headed for the shower. Avantika and Rajesh were ready and waiting for them. Aadvi and Sean made their way to the room.

"Why didn't you guy start?" Aadvi asked.

"We wanted to wait for you guys…what took you so long?" Avantika shouldered Aadvi mockingly.

"Mom and Dad called to wish me, while I spoke to them, Mr. Whitman here took ages to get ready!"

"Tattle tale is what you are Ms.Kapoor!" Sean joined in the fun.

The group finished breakfast and made a move for the beach. On Sean's special request the innkeeper arranged for a special picnic basket complete with imported Caviar and a bottle of Veuve Clicquot Champagne.

As the couples reached the beach they found the perfect spot for picnic. It wasn't too crowded. The weather was a perfect host, cloudy one moment sunshine the next, the breeze played with Aadvi's hair, which she had left open, since Sean liked her hair that way.

Avantika and Rajesh decided to take a stroll on the beach, while Sean and Aadvi wanted to just, observe the waves and unwind.

The solitude and peace...it was just the thing they were hoping for when they left the city's maddening crowd.

He opened the champagne and poured a glass for both of them.

CHAPTER 14

The Romantic Getaway already began weaving it's magic as Aadvi and Sean began talking about themselves.

They realized, despite being madly in love, they knew nothing about each other. This time together bestowed upon them was a perfect way, to know more about each other... and themselves too. Reflecting over the past mistakes and what they had been missing so far.

Sean took her hand and poured his heart out, "Aadvi, I never imagined that I'll find someone like you...I always felt I was missing something but could never understand what? Now I know...a companion like you...it might sound clichéd, corny, cheesy, call it whatever, but it's true."

"Sean, my grandfather used to say, people who can make you smile, make you forget your problems...love them... take care of them, more than your own life, because such people are like rare diamonds...you are that rare diamond for me, you've made me richer in every way."

Sean looked at her with empty eyes.

It broke her heart to see him like that but knew something was eating him from inside, something, which he was trying hard to cover in his smile.

"Honey…what is it?"

"Nothing."

"Come on Sean…there's something that's bothering you for the last few days…please tell me!"

"Aadvi, when I look at you and how happy I am with you… how you love me…I wonder where has this love been all along…when I look at the bond you share with your parents, it makes me feel so empty from inside."

"So your parents…" before she could say anything further.

"They're separated and are getting officially divorced, soon, remember that phone call."

"So that's why you seemed upset at dinner that night!"

"Yeah, my father wanted to meet me to discuss it…" his voice increasingly choking.

"The money, the jets, the cars, all a façade to hide the crap underneath. I've never had a normal childhood, for as long as I can remember, I've seen them at loggerheads with each other…every day was a battle, every vacation was a nightmare…heck, they didn't even turn up for my graduation day, my father was in the sack with his 'personal assistant' while my mother was shopping in L.A. with her friends."

"But Whitman Inc. couldn't afford to let these stories affect the stock market. And everything was kept under the wraps until recently when Dad openly started seeing that bimbo, Cheryl."

"I left the house, didn't want anything to do with them. Neither their money nor this lifestyle…but only and only because of my Dad's insistence did not cut ties with them… since the dwindling image of the Whitman Inc. Needed a shake up and they couldn't afford another scandal on their hands…that the lone successor of Shane Whitman's billion dollar empire, left the house."

"What about your Mom?"

"She's only my mother because she gave birth to me! She was never around while I was growing up. Her lifestyle was always her priority…spa weekends, shopping sprees, exotic vacations…If the stocks took a hit, it would affect her too and the settlement has to be made before the divorce proceedings begin since she has a 20% stake in the textile company."

Aadvi looked at him, weighed down with his sorrow.

"I've been brought up by my grandparents, the only people besides you and few friends that I trust. I have quiet an extended family but I rarely meet them."

Sean looked at the waves…perturbed…turned towards her and apologized.

"I am extremely sorry babes, it's your birthday and I killed the mood…with all this sob story."

"Hey, it's ok, I understand…just take it easy."

She reached for him and hugged him tightly placing a peck on the cheek.
They finished their champagne as Rajesh and Avantika arrived hand in hand.

"Hey guys, mind if we share some of that bubbly?" Rajesh asked Sean.
"By all means my friend." Sean poured everyone a glass.

Sean raised a toast," to Aadvi, my love, without whom there would be no purpose to my life, Happy Birthday love… cheers"

They raised their glasses and drank to Aadvi.

"How about we go to the lighthouse in Montauk?" Sean suggested a change of scenery as the beach was getting increasingly crowded.

"Sure" Aadvi was keyed up

They knocked back the champagne and headed to the car. The lighthouse being a famous tourist attraction was already swarming with people by the time they arrived there.

Still they made a day of it, enjoying the scenic views, clicking pictures, conserving the memories.

Their moods were marred by the weather, which played spoilsport all of a sudden. The clouds had begun to build up, indicating a possibility of showers. They collected the stuff and headed towards the car.

The gang reached the inn and headed for their rooms to relax.

Since the showers were light, Aadvi and Sean sat on the deck for some time to soak in the view and then moved inside as it began pouring heavily.

Aadvi wrapped her arms around Sean, who was seated on the couch, in a contemplative mood.

"Hey...are you ok."

"Yeah, better, wish this weekend never ends!"

"But unfortunately, it has to."

"Do you realize, besides your birthday, it's our one week anniversary?"
Aadvi giggled, "Sean, you are keeping tabs like a girl,"

"But for me it seems like I've known you a lifetime. I always had an image in the mind about the guy I wanted to be with, but never imagined it to turn out to be true and so lovely."

"Aadvi…only a fool would let you go from his life."

Very reluctantly he asked her, "If you don't mind, can you tell me more about…" he paused.

She took a seat next to him.

"Akash…his name is Akash," the saddened expression on her face made him glum.

"Hey I understand if you don't want to discuss!" he tried to be supportive.

"No, No I have to tell you everything…can't bottle up my feeling anymore". She took a deep breath and mustered all her courage, "Akash was a selfish guy, with him it was always…I, me myself kind of attitude…Aadvi, let's play golf, let's go to lunch, Aadvi I want to watch a movie, Aadvi, I can't marry you, I love someone else…" Her tear filled eyes, lost in the time gone by, "And the emotional fool that I am, I actually fell for this guy…his charm and persona, never tried to look beyond that. A guy who was willing to offend his father for his girlfriend who he wasn't even sure would marry him".

Sean listened intently.

"But everything said and done I am also thankful to him… for his refusal led me to opening my eyes to my mistake, the penance for which led me to a whole new world…to finding you." She said placing her shaky hands on his.

He kissed her hands and hugged her, not wanting to let her go, giving her security she needed.

It was almost time for dinner but they didn't want to leave the room, for nothing in the world could take away that moment away from them.

They sent a message across to Rajesh and Avantika that they won't be joining them in their room for dinner as planned earlier.

Aadvi headed for her room and Sean followed her. They lay on the bed next to each other, just lost in each other…they didn't talk; but their eyes spoke a million words in a single heartbeat.

They had bared their souls to each other that day…coming closer physically and emotionally. Just lying there with vacant eyes…clothes on but thoughts and feelings exposed… just floating in the unending sea of emotions.

They lay there for moments that seemed like eternity. The rain heavily beating on the windowpane; her hand raking his hair…his fingers stroking her face, he had never fallen in love with anyone the way he was in love with her…since he never met anyone like her. They ached for more and no matter now much they wanted to control it, the primal urges took over them in an instant as Aadvi found Sean coming on to her. He came closer, kissing her with all the fervor he could muster. So electrifying was the moment that she didn't stop him…but was still reluctant helself…something held her back, she was aroused and confused.

What am I doing? Do I really want to do it; can I trust him so early in the relationship?

Trust…but I came all this way to spend time with him…I love him and he loves me, then why am I resisting it?

Sean could sense her hesitation and stopped.

She was relieved.

"I'm sorry Sean…"

"Hey it's fine…you're not ready, I understand…heck even I am not ready…just lost control in the heat of the second." He felt embarrassed.

He kissed her forehead, got up from the bed, picked up his shoes and made a move for his room.

He looked back before leaving, "Gonna call it a night… goodnight babes and Happy Birthday."

She looked relieved and confused…was it the fact that she kept the promise made to her mother or the fact that Sean so understood, either way she felt comforted.

The next day, Sean greeted Aadvi with his usual energy, deciding not to mention the 'episode' the night before.

Everyone was in a jolly mood at the table. After the breakfast all of them checked out. On Rajesh's insistence Sean let Rajesh foot the bill for his and Avantika's share.

It was time to move back to the city. After checking out they continued to have a look around the town of East Hampton. With the weather holding back, they were able to enjoy the sights.

After a breezy lunch and so much fun they had, the gang headed for the city, back to the mundane brick and mortar life.

Evening traffic in the city was a nuisance as ever, but they managed to reach without incurring headaches or killing someone. Sean dropped them off at Aadvi's place.

Rajesh and Avantika gave her minute with him.

"Hey I am sorry about last night."

"Oh come on Aadvi, you don't need to apologize...don't overthink it" kissing her hand assuring everything is fine between them, "I'll call you later babes...bye." He blew her a kiss and drove off

"Bye."

The three of them headed for the Penthouse looking to get some much-needed rest. At dinnertime, Avantika informed Aadvi about change in their plans.

"Aadvi, we are going to Florida tomorrow. Rajesh's cousin lives in Miami and he is insisting we come and meet him since he has to leave for California in three days."

"What…you can't do that Avantika."

Rajesh stepped up, "We are really sorry Aadvi, I understand you are pissed off at us…but I can't help it Aadvi, my cousin is very close to me and was a great deal of support after Mom and Dad passed away, I can't refuse him."

"Just a day or two Rajesh…please!" she insisted.

"Sorry Aadvi, but we have to go, but we will be back, after all our flight back to Sydney is from JFK," he said comforting her.
Though she was unwilling but eventually gave in.

Avantika and Rajesh left in the evening. Aadvi dropped them at the Airport and called Sean as she left for home.

"Hey babes, I was about to call you."

"Really…what's up?"

"Can you meet for drinks at 230 Fifth at the Fifth Avenue?"

"Yeah sure, any special occasion?"

"Yeah very special…my friends want to meet you."

"Sure, I'll see you there!"

Aadvi reached the rooftop bar and found Sean sitting in a corner with his friends.

He waved at her trying to get her attention in the crowd.

"Hello baby!" his twinkling eyes and warm lips welcomed her.

"Aadvi, meet Lizzie, Jay, Philipp and Joey...everybody, meet Aadvi, my love."

"Hello everyone." she acknowledged everyone as she took a seat next to Sean.

Sean ordered another round for everyone.

Lizzie, who had been constantly staring at Aadvi, asked her, "So Aadvi tell me...are you blind?"

Aadvi was surprised and looked at Sean.

Sean was hysterical and so were the others.

"Don't look so shocked Aadvi, what I meant was, you are such a dazzling woman, couldn't you find anyone better than this jerk on your left?"

Jay joined in the fun, "we were wondering about Sean's latest misadventure? And decided to check it out for ourselves" Aadvi understood that they were pulling her leg.
"Hey, don't you dare say anything against my Sean..." she announced, wrapping her arms around him.

"Oh she's a keeper, Whitman!" Philipp joined in with his remarks.

Though she knew they were kidding, Joey shuts up everyone, "cut it out people, stop being mean to her."

Sean introduced Aadvi to everyone that night, overturning her fears regarding their relationship. Though she might not confide in anyone but after the incident the other night, she became a little insecure…but now she felt safe. Sean was different and not a wham-bam-thank you-mam kind of a guy. Sean on the other hand was happy to see her hit off with his friends since his friends were like family to him.

Lizzie was fashion photographer, who was already in a steady relationship with a Cop, a fact confirmed by Sean when he understood Aadvi's curiosity about their history.

Philipp was the editor in chief, with a small publishing house, run by the Whitman's.

Jay was a writer, originally from London, and now settled in New York.

Joey was an executive with Whitman Textiles and an old batch mate of Sean from his days at the Harvard.

The evening passed quickly. Stories of their friendship were shared, while Sean and Aadvi told them about how they'd met and their short journey so far and what they hoped for in the future.

She was content with the fact that, at least Sean was thinking about her in his future.

While she relished every second of their company, it was already 11:30. Aadvi, took leave from everyone, Sean dropped her off at the door.

"I am so happy you hit it off with them." He was happy and high.

"I am glad to have met such a great bunch of people." Aadvi knew how close he was to his friends and she herself enjoyed their company.

She kissed him goodnight and left for her place. Sean joined his friends back at the roof, as his friends planned to stay longer and drink till late hours.

CHAPTER 15

On her way back Aadvi was immersed in Sean's thoughts and what a wonderful weekend it had been. She couldn't stop grinning even as she entered the elevator with people staring at her.

Tomorrow I've got tell Sean about my plans to go back to Delhi to meet Mom and Dad…oh God, how will he react?

The elevator opened and Aadvi turned towards her Penthouse, where the shock of her life beckoned her in form of a call.

It was her mother.

"Hey Mom!"

"Aadvi!" Preeti sounded depressed as though she'd been crying!

"What happened Mom?"

"Aadvi…Inderjeet uncle passed away!"

Aadvi was flabbergasted…

"But how Mom, what happened?"

"He was depressed since…" she paused a bit, "Akash's refusal…if you understand what I mean!"

'Yes Mom…how's Roma aunty?"

"She's not good…even she's unwell…they both had very traditional mindsets, Inderjeet could never get out of it that he had to break a promise made to your *Naanu* and Dad Both of them took Akash's decision too hard on themselves."

"How's Dad holding up…he was too close to him!"

"He's miserable…in fact I called you to ask you if you can pre-pone your trip to Delhi?"

"Yes Mom, oh this is just so out of the blue…don't worry, I'll be there as soon as I can!"

Aadvi hung up the phone and dragged herself to the bed, eyes burning with tears. Inderjeet's smiling face just popping in front of her!

Did he really take that whole incident so hard?

With a heavy heart, she informed Sean of her plans, the next morning.

"Hey!'

"Hey babes! Why do you sound so serious?"

"Sean, I am going back to Delhi! There's a family emergency and my parents need me back there!"

"What happened? Can I be of any help?"

"No it's something I've got to handle on my own!"

"But what is so important that you've decided to leave in such a hurry?"

"My Dad is really depressed, since a very dear friend, almost brother like, passed away?" After a momentary silence, "I was planning to tell you that, I was going to India in early December, but will have to pre-pone it now, since my mother called in last night!"

"Was he…your Dad's friend…related to Akash?"

Had jealousy seeped in?

"Yes! His father!"

"Are you sure you want to face that guy again"

"Sean! I don't want to, but I do respect his parents like my own…I have to go…and after all we've been through in the past few days, you should trust my decision!"

"Alright…I am sorry…I acted so weird…please take care of everyone, and let me know when you leave!"

"Well I am looking at flight's right now and I can leave in the afternoon."

"Alright baby, I'll drop you at the airport, I'm coming over right away!"

"Sean can I ask you for a favor?"

"Babes…just tell me what you need!"

"Can you take in Amigo for a few days, take care of him?"

"Of course babes, gather his stuff and I'll pick you both in an hour."

Aadvi prepared to leave; she packed her bags all while her mind was flooded with images of the past. Why was that despite being in a near perfect relationship with an outstanding guy, her mind was wandering at this point of time? The uneasiness was too much for her.

Sean arrived at her place, helping her with the bags in the car. She makes a call to Avantika informing her about her sudden departure and another call to Kutty to convey the news of her unavailability for a few days.

They reached the airport, just in time. With a heavy heart and tear filled eyes, she left Sean and moved towards the departure gate. Sean almost felt breathless the instant she left his hand.

But the action she took, was the need of the hour…her family needed her, she had to step up. Somewhere in his heart he too wished he had a family like her's.

She took her seat and began looking out the window as the flight took off.

Bye bye New York...you gave me a lot to cheer about, you changed my life...most importantly, you gave me Sean...see you soon

23 tiring hours later, Aadvi reached Delhi. The driver was there to pick her up. The driver informed her that, her parents were at Inderjeet's house, as Roma was not feeling well. She asked him to drive to the Khanna House.

The thought of facing Akash again gave her the chills. She didn't want to see him, but knew he'll be there and she would have to be civil with him, despite the existing tension between them.

The Khanna residence seemed gloomy after Inderjeet's untimely death. Aadvi entered the house and saw her parents sitting with Roma in the living room. Rajan and Preeti hugged her. Aadvi offered her condolences to a devastated Roma who sobbed uncontrollably.

She sat next to Roma with her arm over her shoulder supporting her. The moment she dreaded was here. Akash walked down the stairs to find Aadvi sitting next to his mother, supporting her in time of need. He seemed uncomfortable; couldn't even look her in the eye.

But he had to face her now. He walked towards her trying to avoid a direct eye contact. Aadvi could see that despite everything he seemed to be...OK.

Is he ashamed, is he sad…can't even be sure of anything when it comes to Akash!

"Hello Aadvi."

She looked at him and without even saying a word she only nodded, acknowledging his presence. He could make out she had still not forgiven him.

Rajan could see how uneasy his daughter was in Akash's presence. He asked Preeti and Aadvi to make move for home. They took leave from Roma and rushed towards their cars so as to avoid further discomfort to Aadvi.

Preeti left for home in Aadvi's car while Rajan drove away in his, to see his lawyer for some legal discussion.

"So how was your flight dear?"

"Tiring Mom…" she was quiet.

"What happened, you look stressed?"

"Whatever I saw today just broke my heart!" she was overwhelmed with sorrow.

"Yes it is heartbreaking to see Roma like this…even your Dad is really depressed, hardly eats, both Inderjeet and your Dad took Akash's decision very hard…though Rajan was still trying to move on after you left for New York, Inderjeet couldn't forgive Akash after that!"

Aadvi was silent...thinking about the chaos that one Goddamn proposal had created. Her heart was even more bitter thinking about Akash.

She heaved a sigh of relief as her phone rang. It was Sean...

"Hey babes! Hope you reached safe and sound?"

"Hey...yeah, I am fine...my mother is with me. We are on our way to home!"

"Was the flight late? You should've reached two hours ago!"

"Had to make a stop first...anyway please take care of yourself and I'll call you later...have a terrible headache right now!"

"Aadvi, love, take care of yourself and let me know if you need me."

Preeti was pleased at least, her daughter had moved on.

Once home, Aadvi went to her room as the helpers took care of her luggage.

"Aadvi, are you hungry dear?"

"No Mom, I just want to rest for a while...I'll see you and Dad at dinner."

"Alright, whatever you want." Preeti closed the door and left a tired Aadvi, lying on the bed with her eyes closed and reflecting on the last 48 hours. She had hoped to come back to Delhi in two months, probably with Sean by her side… and in a happier mood.

Why did I have to come back this way? Sean…I miss you so much!

Back in New York, Sean himself was in a reflective mood, missing her terribly. He had never missed any of his girlfriends before…none of them worthy to be missed. She had brought out that side of him…the emotional side. That side of his character, which he hid from everyone, even from himself by engaging in meaningless, flings with superficial women.

He gazed at his phone, flooded with her pictures from the Hamptons. He missed her intolerably.

Can't get through one day without her…hope she comes back soon

Back in Delhi, Aadvi sat down for dinner with her parents, too upset with what had happened…quiet, blank expression on her face; she played with food rather than eating it. Rajan, tried to break the ice, "so darling how is New York?"

"Great Dad…moving there did a world of good to me!"

"And how's Sean? How was your trip to the Hamptons?"

"It went well Dad and Sean is great guy, I am glad I met him…good things take time."

"I am happy for you dear."

"How are you holding up Dad, I know you were every close to uncle!"

"It will take time but I'll be fine...takes time to adjust to life without your best friend"

"I understand that, but Dad start taking care of your health…"

"Alright Princess, as you wish!"

Aadvi was at ease now, having talked to her father, meeting her parents after all these months.

"So dear, what are you plans…for how long do you want to stay in New York?" Preeti seemed tensed about Aadvi's future.

"Mom…I am having a great time there with the work, the friends, plus with Sean in my life now I have my hands pleasantly full! I don't want to give up on that!"

"So do you plan to settle soon?"

"Mom it's too soon to think about marriage! You know how bad this year's already been; we've lost *Naanu* and now uncle. I am trying to make something of my life, just can't think about marriage at this point of time."

"But do you see a future with him?" Rajan joined in the conversation.

"Yes Dad, I surely see a future and Sean is not at all like the regular guys from the west who believe in dating for dog's age before proposing…can we please let's just end this conversation right here, it's getting on my nerves…I don't want to discuss it further."

She excused herself and bid her parents goodnight and headed for her room. Her room was the same as she had left. But she missed New York, the Penthouse, Amigo and her love…Sean.

Part of her just screamed to get back to all of them.

CHAPTER 16

Aadvi didn't wake up in the morning due to the jetlag and needed the rest considering she'd been crying the night before…missing her days in the Big Apple.

It was almost 1, when her mother decided to wake her up. She entered the room, turning the curtains aside and letting the sunshine in.

"Aadvi darling, wake up, it's already one!"

Aadvi woke up, still jetlagged.

"Mom, where's Dad?"

"He left for the office about two hours ago, he was disturbed since last night."

Aadvi realized she had overreacted last night, which was unlike her, that too about something she herself wasn't clear about!

"I am really sorry Mom, didn't mean to overreact lake that but…"

Preeti stopped her right there, "it's ok dear, don't worry, he'll be fine…he knows you were tired, but we are worried about you."

"Mom you don't need to be worried about anything, I'll handle everything." she assured her mother.

"Now get dressed and meet me downstairs for lunch."

"Alright Mom."

She took a moment to remember Sean and the calls he made every morning to wish her.

As she was about to enter bathroom when her phone rang… she instantaneously knew it was Sean.

"Hello angel, how are you?"

"I am fine my love, I was just thinking about you?" she was in a joyful mood to have heard Sean's voice.

"Oh really…and what was that you were remembering about me?" he wanted to hear more.

"Your eyes…your lips…our hugs and kisses…"

"I miss you too babes…Do you want me to come to India to meet you?"

"Nothing would make me more happy than to see you right now...but I am planning to come back soon."

"Why what happened...I hope he didn't say something?"

"No, nothing like it...I just want to get back to the sane side of things...it's insane here!"

"Alright angel, keep me posted."

Aadvi could sense how forlorn he was without her and she too was desperate to go back to him.

After getting ready, she joined Preeti at the dining table for lunch. She had never been away for so long since her days at the Oxford and Preeti missed her more now, ever since she lost her father. She wanted someone to be with her in the big lonely house. Rajan was busy with work now and Aadvi who shared the workload with him earlier was now settled in a country far away.

Aadvi could understand her mother's loneliness and sympathized with her.

"Mom why don't you come to New York with me...spend some time with there, and meet Sean, once you get to know him better, I bet you all your doubts will be quashed."

"I'll talk to Rajan about it."

Just then, the butler walked in, interrupting them.

"Aadvi mam, Akash Sir is here to see you!"

Aadvi was shocked to the core. She looked at her mother with inquiring eyes asking if she knew, he was coming over. Preeti herself was stunned.

They both got up and entered the living room where Akash was waiting for them. He was restlessly pacing around in the living room. He see's Aadvi walking up to him with her mother.

"Hello Aunty…"

"Hello Aadvi!"

He couldn't look Aadvi in the eye.

"Hello Akash", Aadvi responded coldly.

"Akash *beta*, please sit" Preeti greeted him, "what would you like to have, tea, coffee?"

"Water would be fine aunty!"

The helper was instructed to get water. He continuously glanced at her, while talking to Preeti.

"Akash, how is Roma doing?"

"Well aunty, how do you expect her to be…every single day to see her sobbing like that…just kills me from inside!"

Aadvi was flabbergasted to here such hypocritical words coming from him…knowing he is the reason, the two families were mourning his Dad's demise.

The butler walked in and informed Preeti about a call from the NGO. Preeti excused herself to attend the call, leaving Aadvi with Akash. A few months ago, Aadvi would have been over the moon to find some alone time with him, but today, at this very moment she felt sick to the stomach.

The helper entered with a tray with a glass of water and served it to Akash. After he left, Akash mustered the courage to speak to Aadvi, who was obviously in no mood to even look at him let alone talk.

"How are you doing, Aadvi?"

"I am fine…" still giving him the cold shoulder.

"How are things with you in New York?"

"Great…"

"Aadvi, can we go out for a coffee or something?"

"Why go out, we can have coffee here?"

"I know but I wanted to talk to you alone!"

"What's there to talk about and we are alone…whatever you want to talk about, just go ahead…say it?"

"Aadvi, try and understand, there's a time and place fore everything…I am requesting you as a friend to please give a chance to sort things out!"

"Friend...huh...and you want to sort things out" a hint of sarcasm in her tone, "that's what I want to know...what do you want to sort out? The fact that you rejected me, the fact that my Dad and your Mom are grieving because of you" Aadvi stopped at that, there was so much more she wanted to say to him, but saw her mother entering the living room.

Akash, feeling completely embarrassed now, got up to take leave.

"Preeti Aunty I just remembered, I have to meet someone...I will see you guys later."

He exits in a hurry...Aadvi hoping never to see him again.

"What happened Aadvi, why did he leave in such a hurry?"

"Leave it Mom, don't want to talk about it and I am requesting you please make a decision soon about going to New York, since I no longer wish to stay here and see him again!"

"You are still hung up on that issue...I thought you were sensible enough to move on!" Preeti frowned.

"Mom, Why shouldn't I be hung up on that...his mother is a widow today because of his uptight attitude, my father is depressed because of his stubbornness, he broke my heart, I am living across in another part of the world away from my parents, just to be free from him..." she was on an emotional high as tears flowed from her eyes.

She ran away to her room…the trip was turning out to be a nightmare for her…she longed for Sean…she longed for the solitude she only found in New York and a sense of security she only found in Sean's arms..

That night, after thinking a lot, Preeti decided to skip the New York trip for some time and focus on the things at hand. Rajan's health, the house, she regularly visited Roma to keep her company since her circle was very limited and she only confided in Preeti.

Aadvi didn't hear from Akash after that day. Two days had passed since then; Aadvi was relaxing in the garden with Preeti. It was the first week of November and the warm, morning sunshine, made garden the perfect place to enjoy breakfast.

Suddenly a memorable tune just refreshed her lazy self. She could hear a familiar tunw of Moondance. The music came from behind one of the huge palm trees in the garden. She was intrigued and looked around but found no one.

Her heart said said it was Sean but mind said otherwise.

I think…I think its Sean…no, can't be him…or can it?

She looked around and suddenly two familiar hands closed her eyes from behind. She instantly knew it was him. It was him, it was really Sean. She couldn't belive it.

"Sean…" she turned back, "it's you, Oh my God, I can't believe it."

They stood there, hugging each other for eternity. Their lips ached for each other, but knowing Preeti was right there, they stuck to the hugs.

"I so wanna kiss you babe!" he whispered in her ear.

"Me too my love…but Mom's right there." She murmured back.

She introduced Sean to her mother.

"Mother, meet Sean."

"Hello Sean, Aadvi's spoken a lot about you"

"But how come you are here?" Aadvi was getting increasingly restless to know.

"Well, I decided to surprise you…took the jet and flew here to be with you!"

Aadvi was unable to wipe the grin on her face. Preeti offered him tea, which he gladly accepted, and she left the lovebirds to catch up.
Sean turned back to Aadvi, "Aadvi…baby, four days and I couldn't stand it! It might sound clichéd 'again'…but I can't live without you." He took her hand and kissed it.

"I was missing you too honey!" she grabbed his hand.

"How are your parents doing? Is your Dad better now?"

"Yes he is…I was planning to come back in the next two days though."

"Now let's stay here for sometime…show me around Delhi and we'll fly back together."

"That's the thing…I don't want to stay here!"

"Is something wrong?"

"Sean…Dad's fine now…Mom's taking good care of him…I am not needed here anymore…let's just go!" she sounded aggravated.

"Is it about that guy? Did you meet him? Did he say anything?"

"Does it really matter?"

"To me it does! If he's bothering you, we should take care of it…talk to me, what happened!"

"Well he came here two days ago and wanted to speak to me but I didn't want to, I shunned him."

"So you shunned him, then it shouldn't even bother you, you did the right thing…well I am here now and you don't need to worry about him…rather focus on me, I undertook such a long journey for you."

He made such a puppy-like face that she couldn't contain her laughter.

The helper brought tea for Sean and they chatted away for sometime before it started getting a little chilly, Preeti called them inside. Rajan arrived in the evening and found Sean in the lounge with Aadvi. He was glad to see him and more importantly to see his daughter happy with him.

"Sean, let me go change and freshen up and we'll share a drink."

"Sure Mr.Kapoor!"

Sean's luggage was sent to the guest room. The men relaxed in the lounge with their drinks and cigars while the women looked after the food. Aadvi made sure Sean's favorite dishes were ready in time.

Rajan ordered the dinner to be served early that night since Sean was very tired and wanted to take rest. It meant a lot for him to take care of the needs of his guests and Sean was much more than that. For someone who made his daughter happy and lively, shaking her from the corpse like state she went to New York in, Sean clearly deserved all the attention.

Aadvi was over the moon to have him near her, in front of her. After the dinner, the in-love couple took a stroll in the garden, stealing a moment of passion in the process before heading their separate ways.

"Good night angel!"

"Good night my love"

It was indeed a good night!

CHAPTER 17

It was a great morning the next day. After many months, everyone could feel the positive vibes of the house. It was absolutely tranquil. Aadvi was her chirpy self, Rajan took a walk in the garden with Sean, and Preeti offered her prayers in the temple like always but with her heart full of serenity.

They gathered at the breakfast table and typical Punjabi breakfast complete with *parantha's* and *lassi* was served.

"The food was excellent Mrs. Kapoor!" Sean was impressed.

"Thank you Sean." Preeti smiled back, instructing the plates to be cleared.

Aadvi and Sean decided to go for some sightseeing. They left soon after the breakfast.

Aadvi showed him a number of places like Dilli Haat, Connaught place, etc before they decide to cut short their trip for some much-needed lunch. They craved for sushi and drove down to Sakura at the Metropolitan.

"It's so great to have you here."

"I would've come to moon had you gone there" he said with a foxy smile.

She rolled her eyes, "oh God how cheesy…now that's what I call cliched."

The food arrived and so did a bout of trouble for Aadvi. Just when everything seemed to be going great for them, Akash walked in with a female 'friend' in tow. They were a couple at least it seemed like that, when Akash took her hand and kissed it.

What audacity, he just lost his father and he's back on the dating circuit.

She tried to avoid any kind of eye contact with him preferring to be unmoved by his presence.

But as luck would have it, Akash's eyes fell on Aadvi sitting with Sean. His curiosity beckoned him to see, who she was with. She dreaded him coming over to their table and that's just what he did.

"Hello Aadvi!"

She looked up. Sean was puzzled.

"Hi Akash!"

Oh Hell…The moment of truth was here.

The guy-I-love-the-most meet the-guy-I-hate-the-most!

"Sean, that's Akash…Akash, that's Sean."

While Akash was bemused, Sean looked at him with utter disdain. But still exchanged courtesies. Aadvi felt suffocated and wanted to head back home as soon as possible.

Aadvi's discomfort was evident from her facial expressions and Akash understood that. He moved back to his table. Sean and Aadvi finished their lunch and hurriedly left the place.

While in the car, Sean held her hand, as she looked bewildered, "hey are you ok?"

"Yeah"

"Babes, would you mind if I talk to him?"

"What's the point in talking to him…let's take a break from all this, let's go home."

"Yeah, let's do that."

They drove towards home.

Not a word was spoken for remainder of the journey.

After reaching home, Aadvi rushed to her room.
Highly upset from everything that was happening, she felt queasy, even came down with high fever that night, lying in

her room in a semi-conscious state. The doctor was called and he gave Aadvi the neccesary medication. Her mother put her to sleep and walked out the room, praying in her heart.

Sean was getting increasingly concerned for Aadvi. He found Rajan in the lounge with Preeti and decided to have a talk with him over the issue.

"Mr.Kapoor, I would like to take Aadvi back to New York with your permission. Obviously she has some past issues she's dealing with and those issues are still haunting her."
"So you do know about Akash?"

"Yes I do, for your daughter is so clear hearted, she told me everything from the beginning. And now since she came back, facing Akash is getting increasingly difficult for her… she needs closure. Especially after today!"

"What happened today?"

"We were having Lunch at this Sushi place where Akash walked in with some girl and they were quiet chummy with each other, to be honest."

"So what so you suggest, Preeti?" Rajan seeked Preeti's input on the situation.

"Well Aadvi told me a number of times about her plans to go back since she didn't want to stay here and for her sake I'll permit her to go."

"Sir, I love your daughter and would do anything to make her happy. And I know she'll be better off in New York than here in New Delhi." Sean reassured them of his intentions for Aadvi.

Rajan thought long and hard about the situation and then gave his nod of approval.

In the morning Sean woke her up.

"Good Morning sunshine!" he placed his hand on her forehead to check on her fever.

"Good Morning love!"

"I have some good news!"

"Are you expecting?" she laughed heartily poking her finger on his rock hard abs.

"Ha ha ha…very funny…no time for jokes, I am serious!"

He conveyed her father's decision to Aadvi, who was thrilled hearing the news.

Sean made arrangements for them to fly back in his jet that very night. Aadvi's bags were packed and she was all set to take leave from her parents for the second time in that year and both times due to one man…Akash.

Rajan and Preeti dropped them at the airport. Preeti seemed glad to see Aadvi in a better mood now.

"Take good care of my daughter!" Rajan pleaded Sean.

"Don't worry Sir," he guaranteed with his eyes oozing love for Aadvi.

Aadvi felt secure now that she was going back. Her stress began lowering minute by minute as they took off.

"Sean, thanks or everything…"

"You don't to thank for anything…just happy to see you're ok, now just relax."

And relaxation was the need of the hour, it was going to be a long flight and thankfully they were traveling in his private plane. The $ 65 million Gulfstream G650 bought by his father a year ago was one of his finest purchases. Normally used for his 'sexcapades' it now carried his son who flew across continents for his love.

The tensions of last few days were forgotten in the luxury of the customized plane that soothed them. It had a bed, a bathroom, a closet, a kitchen and a bar. The normal 18-seater plane had to be cut down on the seating to accommodate the luxuries.

Sean got a bottle of Argentinean Dona Paula Shiraz-Malbec. Fine wine and two lovers lost in each other. The setting was perfect.

"Sean, I am sorry, we had to cut the trip short because of me…I know you wanted to see Delhi."

"To see you pleased…what could be more important than that?" His hand grazed her thigh.

Despite all the tension and the drama, somewhere in the depth of her heart, she yearned for him, starved for him and at that point in time, the temptation got the better of her.

She moved towards him, took his glass and placed it on the table next to hers. She wrapped her arms around him…he made her feel protected. He hugged her back with equal fervor. It was a sign of things to come. She pulled him closer to herself, placing her hungry lips on his, for a long, zealous kiss. It was a heady experience for both of them.

"Sean, I would like to lie down for sometime." she exclaimed breaking the kiss.

"Sure love, anything you need." Sean was still reeling from the effects of what had just happened.

After finishing their drinks, Aadvi lead him to the small cabin at the back with a bed. She lay down, Sean lied down next to her… they had been in a similar state a sometime ago and remembered how abruptly it had ended. But tonight she wanted to forget all about that…she didn't care anymore… she was with her man…the most perfect guy she had met. Sean realized what was on her mind when she began fiddling with the lights in the cabin.

But he knew, she still wasn't ready for it.

Stop right away Sean…her emotions are playing with her mind and you don't want her to regret it later on…do you?

In one mind-numbing instance, he was top of her, as the kisses got fiercer.

Don't do it Sean…stop it!

He stopped; that very moment.

"Aadvi…let's not proceed further…" he moved aside, got up from the bed and went out of the cabin. Aadvi was speechless as she was finally at that stage where she was willing to move ahead with him and he left the room again, so unexpectedly.

She went after him begging an answer, "what happened?"

"Aadvi we are not ready for this…I don't want either of us to regret this in the future. There is a time and place for everything and it's neither the time nor the place where I want both of us to become one."

"But Sean…"

"No if's or but's Aadvi, you are overcoming a situation and clearly in a vulnerable state and my conscience doesn't allow me to do something that's not right for either of us at this stage." he sounded a little fluttered, "being born and brought up in a western society doesn't mean I'd jump in bed every chance I get. Sex is not everything."

"Hey, alright…take it easy." she calmed him down.

Aadvi looked at him with pride.

What a remarkable man he is!

Sean converted the two convertible seats in to another bed to lie down. He requested Aadvi to take rest inside the cabin.

For the first time he had a bit of nervy anger for Aadvi.

A few hours had passed after the incident and Sean decided to break the ice. He entered the cabin. Aadvi was sleeping.

Oh God…isn't she beautiful?

He placed his hand on her forehead. She opened her eyes and looked at him with an apologetic look on his face.

"I am sorry babe, I lost my cool!"

"Hey, it's me who should be sorry and not you…I wasn't thinking straight. We should wait till both of us are ready to take it further."

"Yeah we should."

"But right now…I think we're ready for one thing…food!" she exclaimed placing her hands on stomach.

"You are so right…how about some pizza?"

"Would love some, but pizza aboard a flight?"

"There a kitchen on board madam… with a refrigerator full of heat & eat goodies. So what will it be, plain cheese or capsicum & onions or tomato with jalapenos?"

"Plain Cheese for me."

"And something to drink madam?"

"Diet coke would be fine, Sire!"

Sean smiled and went to the kitchen. After some time he gets the pizzas and drinks for them. As they gorged on the food like two teenagers having forgotten all about what had happened a few hours earlier.

After giving it a lot of thought Aadvi too was convinced that they were just not ready to take things further and she had been too impatient.

The normally hellish flight from the Delhi to New York was an unforgettable experience. The time they spent together was precious to them and gave them more insight on how to handle things with each other from now onwards.

They reached JFK where her chauffeur was ready to take Aadvi home. Sean had hoped to drop her and spend some more time with his love but on Rajan's order and to spare Sean the trouble, he arranged the car to pick up Aadvi.

Halfheartedly they let go of each other's hands and headed for their homes. She reached the Penthouse with a sense of satisfaction…she was back where she belonged. Aadvi called up Kutty to inform her of her arrival and then called up Sean to inquire about Amigo who was left in the care of his friendly neighbor.

Sean decided to drop him off the next day. Since she was alone and had some free time on hand, Aadvi, ran a hot bath, changed into comfortable clothing and made a cup of fine Colombian coffee. She caught up on her reading, relaxed her mind. An hour later, she moved to her room, recalling about her journey so far, with Sean and how wonderfully pleasant it was turning out to be.

CHAPTER 18

Weeks passed. It had been one and half months since they'd been dating. Since coming back from India, Sean and Aadvi got insanely busy with their work but managed to find time for each other. Sean's clothing line was about to take off and Aadvi's deal with the cosmetics company came through. But despite all the workload, they spent the weekends reveling in joy of each other's company. Their love had grown by leaps and bounds each day.

As thanksgiving approached, Sean got a call from his father regarding the reunion of the Whitman family at Sean's family mansion in Long Island. His parents and relatives were aware of Sean's latest love interest and were keen to meet her. Despite being hesitant, he decided to talk to her.

One evening Sean was cozying up with Aadvi at his place when, he finally spoke up.

"Aadvi, you know its thanks giving after two days?"

"Yes!"

"My family is having a reunion of sorts…and they want to meet you."

"Why do you sound so stressed?"

"I've told you about my parents right and…" he paused "and…"

"Listen…whatever they have done so far, they are still your parents…you wanted me to get over my past and helped me do it…now let me help you."

"But how?"

"By going for the thanksgiving dinner."

Sean was still skeptical.

"Alright we'll go…but I am warning you…you are gonna meet some crazy people!"

"I'll manage…" she assured him with a smile.

He continued, "but the only sanity you will see is from my grandparents. God Bless them. They were my only support system while I was growing up, besides my friends."

After two days, Aadvi and Sean drove to Long Island to the not so humble abode of the elderly Whitman's. Sean's grandparents, John and Edna; having spent 60 great years together, the couple was very much in-love. From is humble beginnings as a stockbroker to staring his own business, John had done it all while is better half Edna was a soulful singer in a club frequented by John. Cupid struck and John slid a rock on her finger. They lived life to the fullest, traveled the world, and had four children, seven grandchildren and four great grand children. Now leading a retired, undisturbed life in Long Island they looked forward to such family gatherings to meet their excessively busy kids.

Sean and Aadvi reached there before his parents. Sean excitedly takes her to meet them. John and Edna were seated in the study.

"Gramps…Granny!" he yelled entering the study.

"Sean, welcome home son!" John got up to hug him!

"Sean, my boy, so glad to see you!" Granny was all smiles to see her favorite grandson.

Sean introduced them to Aadvi.

"Granny, Gramps I'd like you to meet…Aadvi, my love."

They turned back and saw a girl standing next to the door. In a white cashmere sweater and beige pants, her long, brown tresses were open…she looked every bit the angel.

"Oh my, what a beautiful girl!" Edna was charmed.

Sean was glad to see that his grandparents liked Aadvi. He gave her a tour of the magnificent house. He showed her, his bedroom, is walk in closet, a small study that was specially constructed for him inside the room.

She smiled at how happy he was, proudly showing his books.

"I was very studious Aadvi…" he heaved a long sigh, "I grew up in this house…I've spent some great times here…with them you know…my parents were never around, ever since I can remember, I have always seen them fight with each other." He reflected back on the sorrow-laden era.

"Sean, we'll not talk about it right now, let's enjoy the company of your grandparents…they are such lovely people."

"Yes they are."

Just then Sean was informed, that is parents had arrived… separately, as he had expected.

Donna came alone, while Shane walked in with is arm candy, Cheryl. Donna and Shane exchanged pleasantries that were hardly pleasant. Rest of Sean's relatives arrived one by one. Everyone noticed Aadvi and Sean, and how much in love they were. Aadvi interacted with some of his cousins.

The usually quiet house was bustling with life today,

Edna, got hold of Aadvi while Sean shared drinks with his cousins, "come sit here, next to me…" Aadvi took a seat next to Edna, "you know, you are very special to him," Edna pointed towards Sean.

"Really, you think so?"

"Yes…he's never introduced us to any of the girls and whenever we asked him he always said one thing, 'only if she's special enough' and the way he looks at you is the way my John looked at me 60 years ago."

"What you have is pretty special…Sean's told me about you guys and his parents!"

"Ah…Shane and Donna, what a couple they made, so much in love, so full of life…then things got out of hand when Sean was born. While Donna carried him, Shane started an affair with his secretary; well it was the gold digging bitch that started it all. After the delivery, Donna found out…lost her marbles but instead of divorcing him and giving him an easy way out, she started punishing him, became one helluva spendthrift, raking up bills, paid for by Shane…till date. But one thing they share is their love for Sean."

"Oh my God, does Sean know, he thinks otherwise and holds a long standing grudge against them."

"I tried to make him understand long time ago…but he doesn't want to talk about it."

"Don't worry, I'll talk to him." She placed her hand on hers assuring Edna

The dinner was served as the clan sat down to eat. The finest turkey was laid out on the table. John carved the turkey like always. Donna gave Aadvi who sat right across her, a quizzical look, "so…Aadvi…You name is uncommon, what does it mean?"

Sean suspected his mother's motives.

"It means unique!" Aadvi replied politely.

"And unique is what she is…Mom" Sean took Aadvi's hand and kissed it.

"I am sure she is darling!"

She gets a quick glance at Shane who was being fed mashed potatoes by Cheryl, sitting right next to Donna who rolled her eyes in disgust. More than a frown Aadvi saw sadness in her eyes. She knew something was not right.

After the dinner, she tried cozying up to Donna who sat in a reflective mood near the fireplace…alone.

"Hey Donna, mind if I join you?"

"Be my guest."

Aadvi took a seat in front of her.

"Thank you…"

"For what?" Donna seemed stunned.

"For giving me Sean…your son is great guy, I am lucky to have him in my life!"

"Yeah he is a great guy…but don't thank me…I was not a great mother, never played a part in his life…saw him grow up in pictures while I was away loathing is father."

"No mother in the world is bad…situations and circumstances can be bad but not mothers…there is a saying in India, when God couldn't be everywhere…he made mother, the catalyst to all mankind, the key to the very existence of everything. There is a reason the even Earth is called mother Earth."

Donna was warming up to Aadvi; she looked at her with affection now.

Shane walked pass her, raising a glass of wine in one hand and Cheryl in the other…teasing her.

Aadvi could see the frown come back.

She distracted Donna, "they say time is the best healer… even for a medicine to work, you need to give it time…it'll be fine…meanwhile, why don't you show me around the house, especially your room…I haven't seen that…Edna told me what a beautiful room it was?"

Donna gladly accepted her request as both ladies walked away. Sean who stood near the bar with his cousins looked at them, wondering, what was that about.

Donna showed Aadvi her room. It was a big room, exquisitely decorated with expensive paintings, antique vases and furnished with Oakwood furniture.

"It's a gorgeous room Donna!" Aadvi exclaimed.

"Spent some great moments here" Donna recalled, "Sean was conceived here."

There was a knock on the door. Sean walked in.

"Am I interrupting you two?"

"Not at all, Donna was sharing her stories about the times spent here!"

"Times…huh…what times? When she fought with Dad, how Dad once threw a flower vase at her? How once, they almost came to blows with each other?"

"Stop Sean, please stop it…" Donna couldn't take it anymore and began sobbing.

"Sean, do not speak to your mother like that!"

"You don't understand Aadvi…"

"Sean you once told me, there's a time and place for everything…this is neither the time nor the place…"

Sean left the room in anger as Shane walked in with Cheryl.

He looked at Donna and to everyone's surprise, with a concerned look on his face. He asked Cheryl, to go get a drink. After she left, he walked up to Donna, looked at her, he saw the look of repent on her face, and her tears told a lot of stories. He took Donnas' hand and made her sit on the couch taking a seat beside her.

"Donna, you seem upset, what happened?" He was disturbed.

She wiped off the tears, "nothing…nothing!" she just looked down.

"Hey, stop lying…I know these tears, You can't hide these from me…I know when you are faking your emotions and when you are not."

"Look we've had our differences but we can still talk."

Donna looked up at him and peered into his eyes.

He looked right back at her with the love and concern, which he had for her 30 years ago.

Donna was still a gorgeous redhead and Shane a handsome man. Both were in their early fifties had maintained themselves well albeit for different purposes; Donna, to fit in her expensive dresses and Shane for his 'playful' lifestyle. Despite everything that had happened, there was something left in both of them…for each other. The eye contact was steady.

Oh God! She still looks so amazing…I could kiss her any moment!

Shane realized someone standing next to them, it was Aadvi. Donna introduced both of them.

"Shane, this is Aadvi, Sean's girlfriend!"

"Yes I saw her downstairs…though we didn't get a chance to talk!"

"Well there'll be lots of moments to catch up with me, I think you need to catchup with someone else." She looked at Donna.

He turned his focus back on her as well.

Where did we go wrong Shane?

The spark between Shane and Donna was there somewhere, which needed to be fanned. And Aadvi read the situation well. She knew Donna like Shane and other relatives was heading back to the city soon.

"Donna! Why don't you stay back here tonight? Sean and I are staying back for a night; I would like to spend some more time with you?"

Cheryl walked in with champagne and two glasses. Donna looked at Shane as though asking him a question.

"Cheryl, do you want to stay back, because I realized I got some things to take care off here and I'll be busy!" he peeked at Donna.

Donna looked surprised; Aadvi felt her plan was working.

"Baby, what will I do here, it's as it is very boring…"

"So why don't you take my car and drive back to the city?"

"Well alright…there's a party at Nico's…if I leave now, I'll be there in time!"

"Yeah you do that!" he nodded.

Cheryl left the bottle of champagne in the room, kissed him goodbye and drove back to Manhattan for the party.

Aadvi too walked out of the room on the pretext of finding Sean who had left the room in a rage.

Donna and Shane looked at each other for a few moments and without further controlling themselves engulfed into a roaring kiss.

Aadvi found Sean sitting with John and Edna in the kitchen chatting over a cup of coffee. He was in a better mood now. All the relatives had gone back.

The chaotic day came to an end as everyone retired to the rooms. Sean's room was adjacent to his parent's.

In the morning, Sean along with Aadvi, who was already in a very delightful mood joined John and Edna. To everyone's shock, Shane and Donna came down for breakfast downstairs, hand in hand. John and Edna looked at each other astonished.

Edna asked her son, "Shane you were here last night, no one told me, and I thought you left with that blonde friend of yours and why is Donna still here?"

Sean too looked shocked, while Aadvi and Donna were amused.

Shane raised his hand to announce something, "Mom, Dad, son…I have an announcement to make…" he briefly looked at Donna, "we are not getting divorced, *au contraire* we are getting back together and will be working on our issues."

John nearly jumped out of his seat in joy while Sean almost choked on his pancake.

Donna confirmed the news, nodding happily looking at Aadvi who got up to give both of them a hug.

Sean was still clueless as to what was happening yet he got up and embraced his parents, so did John and Edna.

Everyone was in high spirits to see Shane and Donna together.

Overlooking the fact that it was morning, champagne was brought as they toasted a new beginning for Donna and Shane.

Amidst the frenzy of their patch-up, Donna took her son by the hand to get a chance to speak to her son alone for a moment.

"Sean, I know, me and Shane as your parents have not been exactly the best role models…but rather than pulling us down for that, we were praised and thanked for bringing you into the world…for a certain someone in this room, you are a very special blessing and she feels lucky to have you, hope you feel the same for her!"

With these words Donna looked at Aadvi and left Sean alone to think about it.

After the breakfast, Sean and Aadvi left for home while Shane and Donna decided to stay back for sometime, back in the old house, in their old room, in a quest to find their lost romance.

Once in the car, Aadvi couldn't stop grinning on the way. Sean knew she had something to do with what had happened.

They reached New York in short time. Sean joined Aadvi, at the Penthouse.

Sitting on the couch, enjoying a cup of hot cocoa, she caressed him,
"Thanksgiving turned out to be one happy reunion and you were warning me?"

"I know what you did back there!"

"What did I do?"

"My parents are reunited because of you…I've seen a lot of things since I was a kid, but never my parents together… today…thanks to you, I've witnessed that too." With that he clung to her like a kid to a teddy bear.
Unlike the other times when Sean took care of her…today, it was him who felt safe with her.

CHAPTER 19

After dinner, Aadvi fell asleep on the couch. Since Sean had a key to her Penthouse, he quietly left, covering her with a throw blanket. Amigo was with Kutty and his family again for two days while she was away. Amigo had got accustomed to Kutty's family by now.

The doorbell rang. Aadvi woke up suddenly only to finds Sean gone. She was surprised, as to who was at the door at such a late hour?

She walked towards the door and since the electronic security system was not working properly for the last few days, it had her worried.

Still she braved up and opened the door to find another shock awaiting her. It was Akash on the door, standing with a bunch of Tulips…a sight she was familiar with.

"Hi Aadvi!" he smiled at her.

"Hello Akash!" she was blank.
"Can I come in?"

Half-heartedly she said yes.

He entered the Penthouse.

"These are for you!" he handed the Tulips to Aadvi.

"Thank you." though reluctant at first, she accepted and placed them in a vase.

"You look fabulous!"

She was silent.

He looked around the place, "wow it's a nice place...great views!"

Aadvi looked at him inquiringly and was suspicious of his intentions.

"Come on Akash...you didn't take a 23 hour flight to talk about my place or the views of New York! What do you want?"

Akash looked at her one moment and came closer to her the next.

"Aadvi...I am really sorry for my behavior...what I did to you and to our families is not worth pardoning, but I know you are the bigger person and you will forgive me."

He came more close to her taking her hands in his as he tried to hug her.

"What the hell Akash?" she pushed him away.

"I came here to apologize Aadvi, but…"

"But what Akash…can your apology undo the damage done, can your apology bring back your Dad, can it bring back your Mom's happiness, my Dad's friend, undo my broken heart?"

Akash was still persistent, "No it can't but your forgiveness can give me some redemption…after you left Delhi, I couldn't let go of your thoughts, spent sleepless nights thinking of you, I thought to myself about everything that was wronged because of me…I want to make things right, I love you and want to marry you…marry me Aadvi!"

"You want marry me!" her sarcasm-laden laugh echoed in the living room.

"What about Andrea? Your love, your life…the one you were planning to propose?"

"I did propose her but turned out that she didn't want to get married at all…she had commitment issues…also she was seeing someone behind my back…she was two-timing me!"

"Oh really…serves you right!"

"What?"

"What about that arm candy of yours from Sakura?"

Akash hesitated to answer.

"Well go on tell me your excuse!"

"I met her at a party...but she turned out to be from a middle class background!"

Aadvi scowled at him.

"I knew you were a small hearted person...but a trivial and petty one as well. You've proved me right. You are so self absorbed that you don't understand that your actions could hurt anyone...never giving a thought to someone else's feelings!"

"What do you mean?"

"Forget what I mean...you want forgiveness, ok...I forgive you...but not because you apologized to me but because you broke my heart which led me to Sean..."

"Sean?"

"Yes SEAN...the love of my life!"

"The same guy you were with, in Delhi?"
"Yes."

"Oh come one Aadvi...can you actually listen to yourself right now? You've known him for what...one and half months?"

"I've known you since we were kids…and yet I couldn't understand you one bit! But knowing Sean for a few weeks has taught me, that it doesn't matter how long you've known a person…the time spent together…with each other and for each other is what matters."

Tears flowed consistently from her eyes as she continued, "I love Sean…He's been there for me at every step, he's seen me in my best times and my worst, but you, you left me to face my worst times alone…it was always what you wanted… first you didn't want to marry me, now you do, you were not in love with me, but now you are… why is everything about you, and now when Andrea refused your proposal, your selfish and inflated ego couldn't take the rejection."

"AADVI!" he yelled at her.

"Stop yelling at me Akash! You were the one who wanted me to move on…and now that I have… with a incredible man…you want me to ditch him for what…'you'?"

"But Aadvi at least give me a chance!"

"Akash, I gave you a chance and you blew it. I tried my best but I can't anymore. I think we've talked about this more than enough…now please leave!"

"Aadvi, we can make it work. Trust me!"

"Akash…now you listen to yourself…I can give you my forgiveness but not trust…you've lost it. You were the one who talked me out of the situation the last time saying 'if we did get married, none of us would ever be happy knowing that the marriage has no meaning'…it's just not meant to be Akash, now you need to move on."

She continued, "go home, take care of your mother and find someone who you can love devotedly and selflessly and not according to you whims and fancies!"

"Aadvi, we can still have something…we are from the same family status, we love the same things, and we can still salvage everything we lost!"

"There's nothing left to salvage Akash…not with that condescending attitude of yours…please leave."

Akash walked away disgruntled, his false ego shattered to pieces, only to find Sean at the door, listening to their conversation.

He looked irritably at Sean and then again at a weeping Aadvi who was oblivious to the fact that Sean was there the whole time.

"What does she even see in you?" He frowned at Sean.

Aadvi turned back and found Sean standing there, looking at her.

"I came all the way from India to see you and you insulted me…for him!" the ego started breathing again.

"Don't you dare say anything about Sean."

Sean controlled his anger just about.

"Listen 'pal' if you bother Aadvi again, or if I see you near the building let alone her, I'll knock your teeth off!" Sean and Akash were about to start a scuffle.

"Back off asshole" He pushed Sean.

Sean hooked on on his nose, which started bleeding profusely.

He looked back at Aadvi.

"The guy can't even pronounce your name right and you love him?" Akash covered his nose with his hands.

"Akash...just leave for chrissake!" she screamed with derision.

"You'll pay for it!" he warned them as he left slamming the door on his way out.

"I wasn't eavesdropping on you...I came back halfway from my apartment, since I forgot my keys on the coffee table. I..."

Before he could say anything further, Aadvi ran into his arms.

Amongst the tears and quick kisses, she declared her love, "Sean I've said it a hundred times before...but never felt it the way I do today...I love you, I love you, I love you." She was completely distraught.

Sean, who was equally emotional and passionate, kissed her right back.

He had seen and heard everything from the doorstep. Her love for him, her anger towards Akash was a proof of her loyalty towards this relationship. He wiped her tears, got her water and calmed her down.

He took her face in his hands and gave her a comforting kiss on the forehead.

"Honey, I've seen everything and heard everything… you don't need to explain anything to me. I trust you…but yes, at some point I did fear if you would leave me for him but the way you handled things today with him…I also respect you…from the core of my heart."

"I would never dare leave you, not even for the wealth of the world…I cherish what we have and I would rather give up on life itself than leaving you for someone else."

It was decisive moment, a leap of faith, for both of them. They had just declared their love for each other. Ride ahead was either going to be straight or bumpy. But they were ready for it…come what may.

CHAPTER 20

A semi-chilly November made way for a snowy December. A few days passed since that ominous night. Akash's warning left an impression on Aadvi who was scared for her safety as well as Sean's. She became more conscious. Even for something as small as a trip to the supermarket she called the company car or a cab. Sean wanted her to get her free from the paranoia, shake off her fear.

One night for dinner they decided to visit a local deli near her building. It was two blocks away. They walked to the place despite opposition from Aadvi. But Sean guaranteed her safety.

"So…reached here in one piece didn't we?" Sean joked as they took seats.

"Yeah we did, but let's not jinx it! The guy is dangerous…I don't trust him" she retorted.

"You are freaking out for no reason…relax…by the way hows my arch-rival Amigo doing?"

"Lazy as ever! The weather has taken a toll on his activeness... why I can't blame him even I don't get out of the bed easily, the blanket I purchased a few days ago is really warm."

"Want to share it with someone?"

"Hmm...who and what are you suggesting?"

"It's ok if you don't wanna share your blanket...I am pretty warm too!" he took her hands and rubbed it against his own.

"Oh...stop flirting with me Mr.Whitman!"

They finished the food and made their way home. She breathed easy now that they were almost near her place.

"Sean ...you were right, I was freaking out for no reason."

"When I am with you...you don't need to worry about anything my love." he leaned in for a gentle kiss.

But the moment was cut short by a loud thud. A group of men attacked Sean. One of the attackers hit his leg with a plumbing pipe. Aadvi kept screaming for help but an attacker shoved her as her head hit the ground. She started bleeding from forehead.

The attackers snatched Sean's wallet, watch and Aadvi's purse before driving away in a getaway car.

Aadvi informed 911 and the Sean's parents who rushed to the ER where the medics took him.

The doctors informed them about the seriousness of his condition. Besides being beaten black and blue, Sean had a fractured leg and a broken nose.

Donna and Aadvi were in distress while Shane being a man of contacts made sure the assailants were captured at the earliest. The police arrived to take Aadvi's statement. She divulged all the details of the attack whilst being given first aid. The cut on her forehead was not that serious.

"Can you think of anyone who would want to harm Mr. Whitman?" the officer began questioning Aadvi.

"They took his wallet, watch and grabbed my purse...so maybe they were after money..." she stopped suddenly to mentally revisit the incident.

"There is this man!" she paused.

"Is anything wrong Ms.Kapoor? Do you have a name?" the officer asked again.

"Yes...a man from India, who had been after us, he had warned me and Sean that he'll get back at us."

"What was the reason of the warning?"

"I know him back from India and he came to propose me a few days ago, when I refused and picked Sean over him, he couldn't take it and warned us before leaving my place."

"Does Mr. Whitman know him?"

"Yes he was right their listening to all this!"

"What is the name of this man?"

"Akash Khanna!"

"Do you have a picture or an address of him in New York?"

"I don't know where he lives in New York but I do have a picture of him."

She showed the picture to the officer. He conveyed his analysis of the situation to Shane.

"Based on what Ms.Kapoor has told us, it seems this was calculated attack made to look like a mugging."

As the officers got on with the investigation Sean was still unconscious. Aadvi stayed back with Donna and Shane at the hospital and even called her parents to let them know what Akash had done.

Rajan and Preeti were thunderstruck when they heard the news and knowing that Akash had stooped to such a level.

After a few hours, Sean regained consciousness and found his family near him. The doctor requested them to wait out side while him and his team took a look at Sean. The doctor came out after sometime updating them on the situation.

"He seems better now and his vitals show continuous improvement. But he needs to rest for at least 10-12 days and we'll take further look at the foot from there."

They entered the room. Sean was relieved to see all of them together.

"How are you feeling now son?" Donna placed her hand on his forehead.

"A little drowsy from the medication...Aadvi is that a band aid on your forehead, are you fine?"

Aadvi updated him on what had happened and how he landed in hospital.

"I am fine baby and I am glad you are too...I told you that guy is dangerous and can't be trusted." she reminded him.

"Hey I am ok...anyway we don't even know if it was him... since you told me those attackers took my wallet and watch too."
"Yes they did but I am pretty sure it was him."

"I'll make sure he gets what he deserves." Shane was furious.

"Alright people, calm down. Mom, Dad go get some rest and Aadvi, you please go with them and don't go back to the Penthouse alone. I don't want you staying there all by yourself."

"I am not going anywhere Sean!"

"Yes you are babe"

"No I am not and the discussion is over Mr. Whitman."

"I like your attitude girl." Donna was impressed to see her stubborn son being handled tactfully, "come on Shane, he's is good hands."

"Take care son, we'll see you in the morning."

"Bye Mom, Dad." he looked at Aadvi, "so Ms.Kapoor, you got your way!"

"I always do Mr. Whitman and now I would request you to please close your eyes and take some rest."

"Your wish is my command." he closed his drowsy eyes.

She settled herself on the couch, tired, shaken; the last few hours had been nothing short of scary. Looking at a badly bruised Sean, her anger towards Akash knew no bounds. Hoping to get some good news in the morning, she closed her eyes, hoping to get some rest.

At 8 am, Sean woke up. He saw at Aadvi, sleeping on the couch. She looked like a mythical goddess, resting with her eyes closed.

Oh God…I love you so much Aadvi!

Aadvi woke up to the buzz of the phone. It was a call from her father.

"Hello Princess, how's Sean doing?"

"Yeah Dad, Sean's fine!"

"Have to cops caught hold of the assaliants?"

"No Dad…we haven't heard anything from the police yet."

"Keep me updated and we are coming over to see you guys as soon as possible."

"Alright Dad."

Donna and Shane entered the room, "how are you doing son?"

"Much better Mom…Dad any updates from the police yet?"

"I have an answer to that Mr. Whitman."

It was the same officer, who had earlier questioned Aadvi. Due to Shane's friendship with the mayor, the case was given top priority.

"We were able to pull the street cam footage from where the incident took place and were able to identify the getaway car the attackers used and caught the license plate number. The owner of the car was traced in Queens. We managed to nam him and he led us to others who admitted faking the attack to look like mugging." he looked at Aadvi,

He continued, "Ms.Kapoor you were right, it was indeed Akash Khanna who had paid those men to attack Mr. Whitman."

"Well have you arrested him?" she was eager to hear the news.

"We've traced him at JFK, he was trying to fly back to India, and the officers are arresting him as we speak."

"I am glad you did your job so well officer…now make sure the punk doesn't get out anytime soon." Shane coerced the officer to do his best while making a case against him.

"I second that." Aadvi joined in the rant.

"We can't say anything about that right now." The officer exited the room.

Lizzie and Jay come to visit Sean later joined by Joey and Philipp.

"How are you doing man?" Jay was worried.

"My leg hurts like hell!"
"You look so tired Aadvi…have you been here all night!"

"Yes she has Lizzie…Aadvi I am begging you, stop being so stubborn…please go home and take some rest."

"Let me drive you home!" Donna was equally concerned for her.

On Sean's persistence, she finally went home with Donna to rest for few hours.

CHAPTER 21

Sean got discharged from the hospital in a few days. He was glad to go home although with a plastered leg. Sean's health improved day by day and the plaster was a few days away to be taken off. Thankfully the injury wasn't that serious.

But seeing his parents together, taking care of him, showing love and concern, a sight he had always desired for since he was a kid…a vision made possible by that angel who had come into his life. The innocence of her face and purity of heart just melted his troubles away.

Rajan and Preeti had joined Aadvi in New York to be with their daughter. Having lost her husband and the incident with Akash had shook up Roma so much that she didn't want to stay in Delhi anymore and left for Mumbai, to be with her relatives.

As the weather kept getting colder, Aadvi and Sean cozied up in the warmth of their love.

As it was their first Christmas together neared, the panic to find the most appropriate gift begun. Sean wanted to give her the best and Aadvi wanted to give him something exclusive.

His parents too wanted to do something different since it was their Christmas together in 21 years. It was almost a week to go till Christmas Eve, when Sean pitched a plan to his parents and Aadvi over dinner at his apartment.

"Mom, Dad, Aadvi, I propose we all go to Paris for Christmas and New Year?'

"Sounds lovely," Donna said excitedly, "remember the honeymoon Shane?"

"Oh Yes…" Shane kissed Donna in an instant.

Sean looked at Aadvi, hoping to hear a yes from her as well. But she didn't.

"As much as I would like to go, I can't!"

"But why?" Sean didn't expect her to refuse especially after the recent events.

"It's Christmas time and there is already a shortage of people back in the office, many of them have gone to their homes to be with their families. I can't leave work like that and I don't know if my father will let me."

"Aadvi…Let me speak to Mr.Kapoor…I'll convince him to join us too" Shane insisted.

The next night both families gathered at Sean's for dinner.

Shane took up the topic with Rajan.

"Rajan, Sean's cast will be off soon and he wants to take week off to Paris for Christmas and New Year…we were wondering if you guys can join us too."

"Aadvi, mentioned it to me, but the workload in the office is way too much now."

"Rajan, come on, it'll be a change for all of us."

After much persuasion Rajan relented and gave his nod to the program. The ever faithful and reliable Kutty was again entrusted to run the office and once again Amigo was left in his care. But Rajan made sure Kutty's service was well rewarded.

The three couples took off on 23rd December as planned, on the Whitman's jet. It was a pleasant change for all of them. For Rajan and Preeti it was chance to spend some much needed time together, which they couldn't due to their overtly busy lives now that Aadvi was settled in New York and for Shane, and Donna it was rehash of their Parisian honeymoon 30 years ago. For Aadvi and Sean, more than the change of scenery, spending time with each other was the top priority. The young couple had gone through many ups and downs in the recent past and needed the time off from everything.

As the jet landed at Charles de Gaulle, the six of them dragged their weary bodies to their limo from the Four Seasons.

Their suites were the epitome of luxury. Sean shared the two-bedroom suite with his parents while Aadvi was with her folks in a similar suite. Preeti's reluctance to let Aadvi and Sean share a room prompted them to change the original booking of three suites. But Sean didn't mind so long as Aadvi was with him. With the plaster off, Sean was walking with much ease now but not taking too much pressure.

The elders stayed back and ordered room service while the two lovebirds, decided to have dinner at the one of the classiest places in Four Seasons, Le Cinq since Aadvi fancied fine French cuisine.

"Sean, it was such a worderful idea to come to Paris."

"Babes, I knew sooner or later you'd pat my back."

"So what to you wanna do tomorrow?"

"I have something in mind...don't you worry."

After the dinner, they headed for their rooms. Sean looked at her as they walked the corrridor, hand in hand.

"I am still not full...the food was great but I am craving for a pizza right now."

"Hmm...I am stuffed, why don't you order something in your room!"

"You know your mom could've let us stay together!"

"Yeah she could've but…" Aadvi was short of words.

"Hey it's ok…you are here with me…it's all that matters."

"Let me make it up to you." She grabbed him by his pullover and laid a smooch on his hungry lips.

"Well that pacifies my hunger…won't be needing pizza after that."

"Goodnight love!"

She teared herself away only to be pulled back again in his strong muscular arms.

"On second thought, I am still a little hungry!" Sean playfully insisted.

"Stop fooling around before anyone sees us…let me go now…"

"Alright, but I am warning you…tomorrow you're all mine."

"Uhuh…Goodnight." She waved at him.

"Goodnight babes."

The next morning after some much needed rest and a quick breakfast Aadvi and Sean decided to spend some time alone while the parents were left to catch up, know each other better.

"Both of us have seen Paris before…so what will we do today?" Aadvi inquired

"Not much to see besides the snow-covered streets of Paris huh…let's go someplace else?"

"Yeah, let go someplace else…but where?"

"Alright love…I know just the place, we'll move in an hour, and carry your passport!"

Aadvi was confused at to why Sean insisted on carrying the passport.

"So where are we headed to Mr. Whitman?" she asked him in the car.

"We'll you'll see Ms.Kapoor."

The car headed towards the airport where Sean was flying her off to an unknown destination. Her anxiety and excitement couldn't be contained and she asked him again only to hear the same answer.

They reached the airport and at the check –in counter Sean surprised her.

"We're going to St.Tropez!"
"More like eloping!"

"Don't worry…this is a trip full of surprises baby and I am playing Santa this year, bearing gifts for everybody, doesn't matter if you were naughty or nice!" he winked with a sly grin on his face.

"But why St.Tropez all of sudden? We don't even have luggage...what will we..."

"Shhh...like I said, it's a surprise ...and as for the luggage, we won't need it."

"Hope it's not a nudist camp?" she laughed teasingly.

"Oh it's much better!"

"What about our parents?"

"They'll be fine, now let's rush for the boarding, we are almost on time for the flight."

They hurried towards the aircraft and managed to board the flight on time.

And hour or so later they were in '*magnifique St.Tropez*'; sweating bullets by the time they reached the coastal paradise. One by one they discarded their sweaters and other items, stashed them in a bag they bought at the airport. Since there was no baggage to claim, they made it to the exit where a tall, lean and balding man was there to pick them up at the airport. It was Henri, Sean's friend and a renowned fashion designer on holidays in St.Tropez with his live-in partner, Michel, a seasoned model.

"Henri, Michel my friends how are you?"

"We are fine Sean, great to see you...welcome to St.Tropez and this must be your lady love..." Henri took Aadvi's hand, "enchanté"

"Well Sean your surprise is ready! Let me drop you off at the Marina!"

The Marina...is it really what I am thinking...has he chartered a boat?

And he had indeed chartered a boat. It was a sailing boat, 21-meter, predator 68 with two cabins, a luxurious deck and a crew of three. It was a piece of beauty.

Sean thanked Henri and asked the skipper to take out the boat from the Marina. They were sailing in blue waters before they could think.

Aadvi was mighty impressed and buzzing with excitement but the thought of her parents made her nervous.

"Sean what have we done? Our parents will be worried sick!"

"Aadvi don't worry about anything. I'll explain everything later...now be a darling and open a bottle of wine, come here and pucker up."

It was probably the first time in all these months that she knew him that Sean Whitman was being assertive.

"Wow, never saw the alpha male side of yours!"

"So…do you like it?" he asked her grabbing his wayfarers.

"Yes I do like it…it's kinda sexy!" she moved forward to kiss him.

Unwillingly he broke away from her lips, "Just give me a minute! While I guide the skipper about the trip ahead." he headed off towards the skipper.

He returned to find Aadvi lost in deep thoughts.

"Hello…paging Ms.Kapoor to come back on board!"

"Aye aye captain!"

They opened a bottle of wine, "So where were we…ah the kiss." Sean bombarded her with quick but passionate kisses.

"Sean where are we going exactly and we don't even have luggage?" she poked him again to divulge the details.

"Oh God! For the hundredth time I have it all covered… come here, I'll show you."

He took her hand and showed her around the boat. There were two cabins on board. They entered one of the cabins to find two travel bags containing the latest from the world of Parisian fashion.

"All courtesy Henri DeGarmo…he's one of the best."

"He certainly is!" Aadvi admired his clothes, "so what's next?"

"Well, you are going to take rest, while I am going to arrange us some dinner."

"Let me do that Sean, you need rest." she was concerned for Sean, since too much pressure on the injured leg could hamper his recovery.

"I'll manage babes…now, I am ordering you to relax."

"Hmm…why is it that you sound so sexy while being so dominating."

"I am not trying to dominate you babes…I just need you to be relaxed for the next surprise."

"Alright, I'll stay right here."

He planted a peck on her cheek and left the cabin taking his bag along.

Aadvi was in high spirits; high that surpassed all other emotions. It all seemed oh so wonderful and oh so perfect.

Knowing Sean, she could tell he was planning something big, but what she couldn't think that far…

What could it be…oh stop giving yourself a headache…it could be anything!

Aadvi changed into a flowy, beige maxi.

They say there's a song for every reason and for every season. For Aadvi and Sean, the reason and season were the same…love.

She plugged in the mp3 player, browsed a couple of songs and there he was…Ray Charles romanticizing the moment with, *'I can't stop loving you.'*

She fought herself…resisting the temptation of going out and check out what was happening but couldn't do it as it might startle him and ruin his plans. She was lost in her thoughts when someone suddenly blindfolded her from behind. She knew from the musky fragrance of the cologne that it was Sean.

Aadvi was getting increasingly edgy but was enjoying the rush. Sean took her to the lit up aft deck and opened the blindfold. She opened her eyes to a candle lit table complete with a lavish spread laid out with a bottle of fine pink champagne chilling next to it. The deck was aptly decorated for Christmas for it was Christmas Eve. It wasn't a white Christmas, which he was used to, but there were other things he wasn't used to as well…like being hopelessly in love with a beautiful, down to earth and…sexy woman.

He had changed into more preppy sailing clothes. A white linen shirt and khaki shorts with light brown loafers.

The slow but steady sea breeze coming from the north ruffled her hair and the views of a well-lit and picturesque St.Tropez coastline made up for the awesome scenery.

"Sean it's amazing."

"No…you are amazing!"

He took her delicate hands and led her to the table. He pulled out a chair for her and as she took a seat, Sean worked some magic with his manly hands, stroking the nape of her neck and then gently massaging her shoulders. And by God! He knew all the right points. With every knead she let out a moan. By the time he stopped, Aadvi was almost out of her senses.

"Angel…Let's have some dinner now."

The server poured the champagne as the in-love couple gorged on the delectable French cuisine.

"Sean…thank you, this is all so incredible!"

"You have seen nothing yet babes."

"But where are we going and have you contacted your parents or mine?"

"Aadvi, wherever we are going, they'll meet us directly there."

After finishing the appetizing food, Sean wanted more. The build up was so intense; Aadvi's heart was about to burst through her rib cage.
Sean hinted the crewmember. Aadvi was still clueless about what was to come. The helper turned on the music.

The onus was on Tony Bennett this time, to convey Sean's innermost feelings to Aadvi...oh that beautiful swan, right out of the pages of some fairy tale. He wanted to tell her; how he felt with her and they way she looked that night.

"Care to dance?"

Oh, but your lovely
With your smile so warm and your cheek so soft
There is nothing for me, but to love you
Just the way you look tonight

She lifted her hands as Sean held her.

The soft light brought out the sparkle in her hypnotic eyes; her ethereal beauty was second to none. Her hair flowed lazily in the air so did the dress from Henri which she kept on patting down much to the amusement of Sean.

"I knew you were a romantic at heart but such a hardcore one...hmm, well done Mr. Whitman!"

"Well remember what I said, there's a right time and place for everything...and this is not right but perfect..." after gazing at her for eternity, "how did I get so lucky?"

"No...I am the lucky one...to have found you, I'll be honest, I fell for you the moment I saw you on the dais at that dinner, I knew there was something different about you. You swept away all my fears...yet it took me while to understand...I was in love with you all along."

She became a little philosophical, "Fate has nothing to do with anything…life's outcomes are based on the decisions you take and I am so glad I went for the dinner that night at Nobu with you…Where I met the real you."

"Well, you can take another life changing decision baby!" he stopped dancing, got down on one knee…Aadvi's heart was in her mouth.
He reached for his pocket to pull out a stunner of a ring.

It was a spellbinding moment. Tears stuck in her eyes, just waiting to flow.

He kissed her hand, "Aadvi…my love, the decision you take now will affect both of our lives…And I can't imagine mine without you. The life that I've dreamt with you, is only possible if you take that decision now…so…Ms.Kapoor, will you please be a part of that dream…will you marry me and become Mrs. Whitman!"

She stood pleasantly surprised, her face cupped in his palms, an expression of relief, happiness, shock all jumbled in together. Tears flowed consistently, body shivered a little.

"Yes" she mumbled, he didn't quiet get it, "really?" he wanted a confirmation, loud and clear, "yes" she shouted on top of her voice. Sean was exhilarated as he got up and slid the rock on her delicate finger.
They hugged and kissed…kissed and hugged.

The ring itself was a fabulous 10-carat diamond, solitaire set in platinum. Only the finest for his lady would do for Sean.

They called up his parents who were out for dinner with Rajan and Preeti and conveyed the good news.

The newly engaged couple was on a mesmerizing high, lost in the thoughts about the life to come, wedding, honeymoon, and kids…

The boat sailed near the coast of Le Dramont, a few hours away from their ultimate destination, Cannes, where they were to be joined by their parents.

They held their feelings, fought the attraction, and battled the urges.

"I want us to set a date as soon as possible. I cannot keep my self away from you anymore" he proclaimed as they headed to different cabins again.

So near yet so far!

Aadvi smiled back; she couldn't bear the sting of separation but was happy that her 'fiancé' understood the importance of this separation. But it was only a matter of time, before they got married.

In a few hours Aadvi and Sean reached Cannes where the senior Whitman's and Kapoor's welcomed them with open arms.

It was happening…it was finally happening. The Whitman's were about to welcome a new member in the family and Preeti's prayers were answered. He daughter was settling down with great guy.

Hugs were shared...tears of happiness flowed. It had been a great Christmas present for both the families.

"Mom I hope you are fine since we took off like that?"

"Yeah I am fine! I was a little edgy...but I am delighted now...My Princess is finally marrying her prince!"

She hugged her daughter.

"Welcome to the family son." Rajan hugged Sean.

Donna and Shane followed suit.

"Dad, we discussed it over and we want a small and quiet wedding, nothing too lavish or over the top." Sean conveyed, their plans to his father.

"As you say son." Shane was pleased about his son's choice.

The families celebrated modestly in Cannes but the celebrations carried forward back to the United States. A grand party was in order to announce the engagement. In a few days, Hawaii was chosen as the destination for wedding. Even Preeti and Rajan gave their consent to it.

Arrangements were made to fly down only the immediate relatives and close friends from both families keeping in mind, Sean and Aadvi's request of a small gathering on the wedding day. Two receptions were intended; one in New Delhi and another in New York. Akash's mother Roma was invited on Aadvi's request as she still respected her enough, despite whatever her son did.

Avantika who had flown in from Sydney again, was her maid of honor and Aadvi's cousins were the bridesmaid's.

In no time the wedding day arrived. The arrangements were made at the most lavish beachside resort in Hawaii. A four-pillar altar adorned with white and pink roses, was set on the beachfront at sundown.

The bride looked exquisite in a pearl colored wedding gown and a bouquet of white roses accompanied her. She looked like an angel descending from heaven as Rajan walked Aadvi down the aisle.

Memories of her childhood fresh in his mind, like it was just yesterday that she took her first steps… when he dropped her off at school on her first day…the time when she won her first prize…her first play…her graduation. Rajan stopped at the altar looked at his daughter, "All the best Princess!" he embraced Aadvi with tears of joy rolling down his eyes, as he gave her away.

Sean who looked dapper in light silver three-piece suit was awestruck by the flawless beauty of his bride. Joey was the best man while Sean's cousins and other friends took the roles of the groomsmen and the ushers. Amigo and Romeo were present at the altar as well.

Sean passed an endearing smile to a blushing Aadvi as she stepped on to the altar. They were moment's away form starting a new life.

The minister began the impending ceremony.

The guests eagerly awaited the vows, which the bride and groom had prepared themselves. What Sean and Aadvi meant to each other were more than what a few words made from 26 alphabets could express.

"Aadvi, the day I met you, I thought I met and angel, I wasn't even sure if I wanted to know you more. You were like a dream and I didn't want to open my eyes to the reality where I would find you gone…but you woke me, made me realize that you were not a dream, but a beautiful reality…I promise you to be the best husband ever…because you my love deserve only the best. I promise you, that I will love you till my last breath"

He put the ring on her trembling finger.

"Sean, as a little girl I used to envision in my mind, what my prince would look like but the picture was always colorless; my life was colorless…until you came along, filling it with the rainbow of your love and care. Today, we promise each other not to dwell upon the past as we stand here in this wonderful present and look forward to a bright future…I promise you that I will love you till my last breath."
She slid the ring on his finger.

The ceremony concluded to a rousing applause as Mrs. And Mr. Sean Whitman took their first steps into marital world, sealing it with their first kiss. As the sun set on the beautiful Hawaii, their glittering love, lit up the beach.

The celebrations began with elan. It was a wondorus occasion for both families. Speeches were given, stories were shared, the world suddenly became smaller, as the two families became one. Tony Bennett himself performed for the couple for their first dance on Shane's request.

Memories of them in a lovelorn state for worthless people were a thing of the past and faded away from their minds with each passing moment. Finally they were in each other's arms.

Sean looked at her, admiring her infallible beauty…gazed at her long and hard, "You look so enticing right now."

"Wait till you see what I am wearing underneath." she tantalized him.

He prodded his lips against hers.

"What is it?"

"Something special that I had Henri made for me…for you…for us."

"Hmm…So Mrs. Whitman, what do you think…we ditch the crowd and I let you gratify me!"

"I think it's a great idea Mr. Whitman but what do you have in mind?"

"Well…a lot actually, but let's get out of here and I'll tell you all my plans." Wickedly grinning from ear to ear.

She requited his mischievous grin with an equally suggestive one.

He grasped her tender hand, grabbed a bottle of champagne as they left everyone behind to cherish their first moments as husband and wife, to create new memories and build their nest of love. No one could stop them today, even if they wanted to.

They had waited far too long...resisted the urges far too long...for this moment. They deserved to all the solitude in the world, after all they had earned it, whilst finally finding the treasure of true love.

Love...better late than never.

GLOSSARY

Naanu / Nanna – Common Indian name for maternal grandfather

Naani – Common Indian name for maternal grandmother

Yarra – (Punjabi) Friend/Pal

Prah- (Punjabi) Brother

Tikka – Barbequed Appetizer

Kebab – Grilled Appetizer

Puttar – (Punjabi) Son

Bahu – Daughter-in-Law

Jee Aya nu – (Punjabi) Most Welcome

Desi Ghee – Hommade Clarified Butter

Dal Makhani – A Punjabi delicacy, cooked whole Black Lentils and red kidney beans, with a hint of white, unsalted butter or creme.

Kesari Kheer – An Indian Dessert, Saffron flavored rice pudding

Aloo Parantha – Indian bread stuffed with Mashed Potato

Moi – (French) Me

Beta – Son

Au Contraire – (French) on the contrary